W9-BMX-020

SHELTER ISLAND

The Song of Fridorfold Trilogy

Book One

JOHN PAUL TUCKER

Brownridge Publishing

Library and Archives Canada Cataloguing in Publication

Tucker, John Paul, author
    Shelter Island / John Paul Tucker.

(The Song of Fridorfold trilogy; book one)
Issued in print and electronic formats.
ISBN 978-1-988856-02-5 (softcover).--ISBN 978-1-988856-03-2
(PDF)

    I. Title.

PS8639.U3245S54 2018   jC813'.6   C2018-
903245-6

                                              C2018-
903246-4

Cover design by John Paul Tucker

To Irene:
First in the Song who taught me to sing.

SHELTER ISLAND

THE FAR FELL

ARAFEN

HUSGARD

THE FREAWIND

WATCHER'S WOOD

THE GOLDEN FIELDS

THE MUNA MOUNTAINS

THE GREAT WASTE

VULTON CRAGS

SOLTIN MYRR

THE MIRROR SEA

FRIDORIAN PASS

VANGORFEN

VANGORFOLD

Cast of Characters

Cary: Older brother to Clarisse and
 Gregory. The Birdfolc name him Brador
 Halor, meaning Hasty Hero.
Clarisse: Middle sister to Cary and Gregory.
 The Birdfolc call her Arithi the Brave.
Gregory: Younger brother to Cary and Clarisse.
 The Birdfolc call him Aevi, the Seer.

Folc Loyal to Husgard

Mandwar: Owl leader of Husgard Hellir.
Fyrndagas Underdel Dearth: A cantankerous
 though brave rat of unknown origin, loyal
 to Mandwar and Fridorfold.
Adarel: Former leader of Husgard. A singer of Ellri.
The Gildenhyrn: Raptor warriors of Husgard.
Gren: A clever warrior leader of the Gildenhyrn.
Ofost: The fastest warrior of the Gildenhyrn.
Vaskar: A brave Gildenhyrn Captain.

Folc Loyal to Vangorfold

Blodcroew: Also known as Wisefaest, an ancient
enemy to Fidorfold. Whereabouts unknown.
Harfan: Leader of Vangorfold Stronghold.
Scrim: Harfan's spy and Second in Command.
The Dreygar: Fierce Vangorfold warriors.
Vultori: Vultures in league with Harfan.

Other Names to Know

Raven Wing: A solitary and mysterious raven.
Birdfolc: Birds descended from Fridorfold.
The Ellri: An ancient order of Singers.
Ascentor: Prophesied as co-leaders of the Birdfolc
in anticipation of the new Fridorfold.
Firegast: A Spirit Bird of the Ellri.
Folclaguhas: Day of court when Birdfolc are judged.
The Lost Veil: A veil of turbulent, impenetrable fog.
Wyrm: A flying serpent of legend.

Places

Fridorfold: An ancient community of Birdfolc & Earth-dwellers, a kingdom in waiting.

The Fragile Lands: The sibling's homeland, the last inhabitable continental island of this earth.

Shelter Island: An island created by the Ellri as a refuge for Birdfolc.

Husgard: Stronghold of Birdfolc loyal to Fridorfold.

Vangorfold: Stronghold of Birdfolc sworn to Husgard's destruction.

The Golden Fields: A vast field of golden grass.

Soltin Myrr: A dangerous bog.

Vulton Crags: A high plateau home to the Vultori.

Fridorian Pass: An open, unprotected swathe of land.

The Far Fells: Inhospitable land north of Husgard.

The Freawin: A river running from the Muna Mountains to the Mirror Sea, bordering the Golden Fields.

The Watcher's Wood: A large stand of pines controlled by the Gildenhyrn.

The Mirror Sea: Surrounds the island. It always steers travellers back to the island.

One will arrive at a place
which makes the journey home
by any former path
impossible

J. P. Tucker

CHAPTER ONE

The Pouch With The Golden Thread

"It's mine," said Gregory, his older brother edging peril-ously close to his small pouch, drawn tight with a golden thread.

Huddled over the dining room table, Gregory cupped his hands over the pouch and pressed one eye against the gap between his overlapping thumbs and fingers.

"We know it's yours," his sister Clarisse assured him. "We just want to see what's inside."

Cary crossed his arms in front of his chest, stifling his impatience. "Open it yourself if you don't trust us," he said. "We'll just look over your shoulder."

"Promise you won't take it first," said Gregory, hands stubbornly braced over the pouch, his large eyes searching his brother and sister's faces.

Cary weighed the intensity of Clarisse's glare. "All right," he conceded. "Open it."

Hiding from Cary and Clarisse at a nearby park the day before, Gregory had found the pouch nestled in the remains of an old tattered nest beneath the branches of an enormous spreading oak. The pouch resembled a small sewing purse, one that might accommodate a single thimble, yet not so small as to hide from the ever-searching eyes of Gregory. The finely woven pouch was strong, neatly constructed and finely embroidered with a single golden feather, a feather so artfully sewn that Gregory could scarcely distinguish one thread from another under a magnifying glass.

Gregory struggled to worm his slender pointing finger into its tight opening.

"Remember. You promised," he said, convinced more than ever that Cary would snatch away his fairy pouch.

Watching over eight-year-old Gregory was like keeping track of a stockpiling squirrel—non-stop, and non-paying. The arrangement was another non, a 'non-negotiable'. The reason? Their parents, both anthropologists of a sort, were, according to Clarisse, 'obsessing over' a recently discovered artifact at the FAA, the Freeton Antiquities Authority. The discovery was supposed to be, in their parent's words, 'an extremely important piece in the puzzling early history of their homeland'. Important or not, the find had, as Cary claimed, turned them into 'latchkey kids.'

"Just open it," said Cary. "We promised, didn't we? We won't take it."

Gregory wormed his other index finger into the pouch. He ventured a gentle tug. The golden thread released its grip, and the small drawn closure spread open.

Clarisse placed a plate in front of Gregory. "Here," she said. "Empty it onto this."

Gregory turned the pouch over and shook it. Nothing. He shook it again: nothing, not a pip.

"Maybe it's empty," said Clarisse.

"Put your finger into it to see if anything's there," said Cary. "You never take this long when you've got your gummy little fingers in my stuff."

Gregory inserted a finger into the pouch and wiggled it. "I feel something."

"Let me turn it inside out," said Cary.

Gregory surrendered the pouch to Cary. "Don't break it."

"You can't break a pouch," Cary said, examining the pouch.

"Yes, you can," Gregory insisted.

"No, you can't," said Cary. "You can tear it or stretch it, or whatever, but you can't break it."

Cary exaggerated stretching the pouch, then pretended to swallow it. He showed two empty hands to Gregory.

"Give it back," demanded Gregory.

"Just be careful and don't break it, Cary," said Clarisse, choosing not to add Professor to avoid another of their heated clashes. Quarrels ended the same way: Cary storming off, Gregory crying, and Clarisse left to single-handedly mend the shredded remains of everyone's wounded feelings.

Cary held the pouch over the plate. He positioned his index finger at its bottom and curled the pouch over his fingertip to his middle knuckle like an inside-out finger glove, Gregory protesting every step of the operation. Three golden feathers flipped down onto the plate.

"There's something else," said Cary, reaching for a sharp pencil. Applying its tip, he teased a small tube of paper off the side of the pouch onto another plate. Three heads hovered over the small paper roll.

"I think it's a scroll," said Clarisse. "Let Gregory unroll it."

Cary groaned.

"His fingers are smaller," she added.

Cary slid the plate closer to Gregory, with a generous helping of smirk.

After several attempts, Gregory found the edge and unrolled the tiny scroll.

"Clarisse, get the magnifying glass," said Cary, his nose an inch above the parchment. "It's in the pickpocket's room."

"I'm not a pickpocket," protested Gregory to the back of Cary's head.

"What's wrong with your legs?" chided Clarisse half-heartedly. Wouldn't she inevitably be the one to fetch the magnifying glass anyway? "And what happened to please?"

Clarisse left the dining room. "Dictator."

"What did you say?" called Cary.

Clarisse returned and smacked the magnifying glass into Cary's hand.

"Frigerator. It was on the refrigerator."

Ignoring Clarisse's rebuke and nudging Gregory's head out of his view, Cary hovered over the little scroll, steadfastly propped open by Gregory's trembling fingers.

"I can't see," complained Gregory.

"Something's written here," said Cary, "but I can't make it out."

Clarisse curtsied with exaggerated gratitude and extended her hand. "If your highness will allow a lowly peasant to try."

Cary dangled the magnifying glass over Clarisse's

hand. She refused to take the bait, so Cary rolled his eyes, dropped it in her hand and resumed his examination of the three little feathers on the other plate, Gregory on guard.

Clarisse hovered over the tiny artifact the same way her parents would have conducted their research. The letters on the scroll were written in the same spidery golden threads of the embroidered feather on the pouch.

She hesitated to check a word.

> *Three fair feathers travellers are,*
> *Bearing friends or foes afar.*
> *Bound together, by bearers three,*
> *Summons three bearers to bear ye.*

"It's a riddle," said Gregory, his eyebrows climbing with each new revelation.

"Maybe," said Clarisse, who had recalled a passage from a story she had read. "It sounds more like an enchantment."

"Travelling feathers?" mocked Cary, who had coaxed each feather to its own spot on the plate. He picked up two feathers and mimed them beating in the air. "Without a bird? It's a riddle. The pickpocket's right."

"I'm not a pickpocket."

"I wonder who the bearers are?" Clarisse asked herself aloud, ignoring Cary's challenge.

"We should put the feathers somewhere safe so we don't lose them," said Cary.

"They're mine," piped in Gregory.

Clarisse shot Cary a wide-eyed reproach.

"You'll lose them," Cary said, replacing the feathers on

the plate. "Like you lose everything."

"I won't," Gregory answered, sure Cary was going to take the feathers anyway.

"Then where's my gyroscope?"

"I don't have it," answered Gregory, appealing to Clarisse. "What's a gy-yoscope?"

"GyROscope. I know you don't have it," answered Cary, taking his case to Clarisse. "Cause the pickpocket stole it and then he lost it."

"I'm not a pickpocket," answered Gregory, louder this time.

"You should at least put the feathers back into the pouch," said Cary, reaching for one of the feathers.

What happened next was like falling off a ladder, exactly at that point when the ladder has tipped beyond any hope of return.

Convinced that Cary was going to take all three feathers, Gregory snatched one, loudly reminding Cary and Clarisse that the feathers were his. Clarisse, worried that the feathers would be lost or destroyed, took hold of another. Gregory grabbed Clarisse's hand, lost his balance and tipped on the edge of his chair. A feather in one hand, Cary reached out with the other to rescue Gregory. In the excitement, Clarisse grabbed the arm Cary sent to rescue Gregory.

For one brief moment Cary, Clarisse, and Gregory were in each other's grip and holding a feather. The conditions of the enchantment were met.

Grey fog spewed from the pouch, poured over the edge of the table and covered the floor. It enfolded Gregory's feet, as if he were standing in a cloud. The thick rolling mist swirled up and encircled the accidental conjurors as it ascended the walls. The dining room was blotted out.

"What's happening?" shouted Cary, who had cupped his hands around the pouch to no effect.

Clarisse clutched Gregory.

"You're pinching," complained Gregory, waving his free hand through the thick fog setting it aswirl.

Clarisse pulled back Gregory's hand. "Don't touch it."

The lighter, thinner side of the cocooning fog drew their bewildered eyes to fathom the grey mist. A ball toss away, far beyond where the wall of the dining room should have been, soaring as if in a mirage, was a large bird. It was searching for something. It pierced the muted fog with a shriek and banked.

"Cary, it's seen me!" Clarisse shouted, her eyes locked on the bird. "It's going to attack!"

Two other birds shot out of the grey fog and joined the first. The lead bird would reach Clarisse in a few wing beats.

The three birds of prey glided to within the toss of a coin and then sank out of sight in the sea of fog.

Cary stretched forward toward the far edge of the table. "I think they're gone."

Three raptors, hooked talons and threatening beaks leading, swooped up from the table's edge in a burst of splayed feathers on outstretched wings. Cary stumbled back into Clarisse and Gregory.

Stalling in midair, the three large birds lightly dropped their feet and executed flawless flat landings on the polished wooden table, their talons neatly hooked over the edge. All three wore decorated helmets and golden mail fashioned like feather scales. Their stares were grim and defiant.

Clarisse pulled Gregory farther away from the birds' talons. Cary reclaimed his legs and stood in front. The fog retreated as if the birds had scattered it with their wings, allowing the dining room to reclaim its place. The dining table, normally no higher than Gregory's waist, had unaccountably grown out of reach of even Cary.

"What have we done?" erupted Clarisse, her arms wrapped around Gregory, who had now stopped crying and was watching the birds with intense interest.

"What you have done," said the largest of the three raptors, "is summoned us; and so we have been sent, sent to bear you..."

"It was an accident," interrupted Clarisse, already worried about cleaning up the dining room before her parents got home. "You have to leave. You can't stay here, and you're scratching our table."

"We have been summoned. We have been sent. In bearing you hence lies our duty," answered the largest raptor. No one, human or otherwise, had spoken to Clarisse or Cary with such authority.

Ignoring Clarisse's pleas and sidestepping Cary, Gregory presented himself to the birds.

"I want to go."

The smallest of the three towering birds swooped down and in one deft trick had Gregory straddled and strapped over her shoulders. The bird launched Gregory from the dining room into the kitchen and under the sash of a wide, half-open window.

"You can't take him," protested Clarisse. "He's too young. I look after him."

"He has chosen," answered the largest bird.

"Then I'm going too." Clarisse stepped forward. "He

can't go alone."

The second bird swooped down. Before Cary could intervene, Clarisse was astride her transport. In a flutter of wing beats, she was gone.

Cary squirmed under the raptor's piercing gaze. His sister and brother were gone. Cary clenched his jaw. He had to follow.

CHAPTER TWO

Through the Veil

Their legs yoked over the working shoulders of their golden-armoured escorts, Cary, Clarisse and Gregory swept into an expansive blue sky, the alarm of the whirlwind chased away by the thrill of flying.

Bent forward on the largest of the three birds, Cary had gripped a braided harness around the raptor's neck. Gregory was strapped on his bird's back like a knapsack. He was asleep. Clarisse, her eyes clamped shut, had leaned forward like Cary, but had clasped her arms around her bird's neck.

"If you strangle me," rasped the bird under Clarisse, "you shall do us both harm. Take hold of the tethers."

Clarisse released her grip. Not yet daring to open her eyes, she blindly felt for the tethers.

"Your consideration is appreciated," said the bird.

Clarisse shouted against the headwind, "Where are you taking us?"

The large bird under Cary answered. "We are escorting you and your brothers to Shelter Island."

"Shelter Island?" Cary opened his eyes. "We can't go to

an island. We have to make dinner for Gregory."

Cary had never plotted Shelter Island on a school map, nor had he helped very often in preparing dinner.

"Your brother will be well fed," snipped the bird under Cary.

Cary peaked down over his bird's shoulder and closed his eyes again.

The winged escorts and their mounts flew on in silence, climbing high over the children's home, the expansive Fragile Lands, the one known inhabitable continent. At a time now lost to old books and dusty tombs, much of the planet had been ravaged by drought. The thirsty patches that survived were devoured by hungry wildfires. Floods washed over the scorched landscapes, but did not recede. In a single generation, the sudden rising of the oceans submerged greater parts of continents. Remote mountain ranges and high plateaus spotted a boundless sea like the bony spines of amphibious dinosaurs, most too small, too barren or steep to cultivate. If other life-sustaining land-masses existed, the lost civilizations would be thousands of miles away, across unnavigable, tumultuous seas.

Clarisse remembered reading somewhere that hundreds of years ago when the inhabitants of the Fragile Lands arrived in ships they found a race of intelligent birds and shared the continent with them. Now, most people living on the Fragile Lands did not believe in talking birds or an early civilization of birds and people.

This is going to change everything, thought Clarisse.

Clarisse willed her eyes to open. Far below, reduced to a tiny model she could cover with her hand, was the capital city of Freeton. She followed the landscape west as far as the Giant's Table. Clarisse picked up the trail of

Little Brother, a winding river that threaded across half the continent before emptying into the sea at a port city situated on the rim of the Giant's Cauldron.

Clarisse swallowed down the knot in her throat and tucked her chin under her right shoulder. Far below, the expansive Oakenfen, a lore-laden forest of tall old trees, rolled away like a plush carpet of moss. The Oakenfen's roots, it was said, though few believed it, spread under the the Fragile Lands like a giant tangled mat, so thick it kept the whole continent afloat.

Twice Clarisse had seen the Fragile Lands from the height of the Giant's Table, but no view could compare with the vision she was surveying now: the vibrant myriad forest greens, the multicoloured quilts of farmland, the dramatic changes in elevation, all the while the wind whipping through her hair.

Cary was staring into the spray of feathers on the nape of his bird's neck. Plotting something, maybe an escape once the birds land, thought Clarisse.

Once their transports headed out over the Endless Sea, Cary clung to his bird like a crab on a rock.

During tireless strong sweeps of his wings, the striking bird of prey in the lead hunted the skies with his bright, intelligent eye—wise even, like a ship's captain fixing his position.

The large armoured bird cocked its head and made two light chirps, interrupting Clarisse's thoughts.

"Lie forward. Wrap the tethers around your wrists," he ordered. "We must pass through the Veil."

The three birds stretched their wings and banked toward a gathering of murky grey clouds.

No bird would fly into a storm like that, thought Clarisse, but on they pushed.

The cloud approached as thick as her grandmother's quilting cotton. Unsettled humid drafts brushed their faces. At a hundred yards, the massive grey cotton wall loomed in their way like a bulging cliff.

The trio of travellers drew nearer. It was not a cluster of storm clouds at all but a billowing wall of dense grey fog, churning like the rolling sides of giant tangled snakes, and the birds were going to fly straight into it.

"Brace yourselves," ordered the largest bird.

Clarisse closed her eyes and held her breath. She felt one, two more downstrokes of her escort's wings. Then it struck. Blasts of wet wind laced with needling ice pellets ripped into her hair and stung her face, as if she had dived into nettles. She released her right hand to shield her eyes but had not covered her eyes for a wing beat before the lashing stopped.

Clarisse opened her eyes. The turbulent dark grey mass had been forced back in every direction, giving way as if the travellers were flying inside an invisible bubble.

In this way the company continued their passage, a tendril of dark mist occasionally snaking into their sanctuary but breaking up and dissolving before coiling round the travellers. Clarisse wondered when the boiling grey murk, like the same fog that had made a cottony cocoon of their dining room, would finally collapse and swallow them. But like coming to the end of a long tunnel or waking from a nightmare, the dark, knotted bands of fog unwound. Gaps opened. Light, like the first streaks of light after a passing storm, struck their faces. The company flew on till every murky tendril had withered away in light grey whispers.

The blue sky had returned, dappled with puffy white clouds. Below, shimmered a tropical turquoise sea surrounding a large island.

"Cary," said Clarisse, hardly able to breathe. "It's a secret island." Not one of Clarisse's teachers had mentioned anything of an island near the Fragile Lands.

Cary did not respond. His eyes were too busy feeding on the rich landscape. He was fixed on a range of mountains, stretching into the horizon.

"The Veil has played us a trick," said the largest raptor under Cary. "We are over Vangorfold."

"We have been spotted," said the bird under Clarisse.

The larger bird under Cary screeched twice. The birds bearing Clarisse and Gregory immediately rolled to either side. In seconds, Clarisse and Gregory had shrunk to small distant dots.

Cary's mount brought in his wings and dived. The sudden drop created such a fierce wind that Cary had to bury his face in his bird's shielding neck feathers.

"Take hold," commanded the bird needlessly. Cary already had a white-knuckled grip on the tethers.

His world rolled. He squeezed his eyes shut, hoping to wring the topsy-turvy world out of his head. He was mounted on an out-of-control, looping roller coaster. The nausea that had been teasing his stomach swelled into an unstoppable wave. The bird plunged through a treed canopy. Cary passed into warm green light. He swallowed hard to keep a lid on his churning stomach.

"Dismount. Wait here till I return," said Cary's breathless escort. "Talk to no creature. Hide yourself."

Cary slid off the bird onto a high branch of what must have been the largest tree in the world.

"Hide!" The bird thrashed up through the tree's leafy canopy.

Cary stood on the branch and waited, the quivering canopy of leaves offering no sign of his escort's return. When the minutes strained longer, the moment when he had coned his hands around his mouth to shout for help, shrill bursts of high-pitched shrieking tore the silence. But above the tangle of high branches not a single bird streaked through the small patches of blue and white sky.

His neck in a stitch, Cary lowered his gaze and massaged his cramped muscle. The rounded top of the tree branch on which he was standing had a girth as wide as Cary's outstretched arms. In measured steps, he walked half the length of the branch and sat with his back to the trunk, hidden from the sky. He waited.

"Why hasn't the bird come back?" Cary stretched out on his stomach and peeked over the rounded lip of the branch. The distance to the ground set his head in orbit. He was stranded in the top branches of the tallest tree he had ever seen. If he called for help, who would answer? He leaned back and sat against the trunk.

The whispering leaves fluttered into his thoughts. *In the span of an hour, poor boy, you have been forced onto the back of a talking bird, shot into a hurricane and dumped in my arms. And where are your sister and brother?*

The tired sun was drifting toward the horizon. The armoured bird had not returned. The branches below, his only escape, laddered down at dangerously wide intervals.

Perfect climbing tree, Cary thought, *for a giant.*

He finally yielded to his lofty prison and returned to the trunk. He drew up his knees and watched the galaxy of flossy seed-down rising and falling in narrow shafts of warm sunset light, waiting for his rescuer.

The lush green world darkened. Not a chirp from above, nor the crackle of a twig below invaded the quiet of his high perch.

Cary replayed the dramatic scenes of the afternoon wreathed in the gentle whispers of the tree until his wavering eyelids surrendered and he fell asleep.

CHAPTER THREE
Kidnapped

At sunrise, Cary was sitting with his back against the tree. He had spent a wakeful night, wary of tumbling off the branch in his sleep. Every muscle uttered a complaint.

"So what am I supposed to do now?" Cary said aloud as he stood and stretched. "Where's that stupid bird?"

In the silence of his unanswered question, a conversation a notch above a whisper fell through the leaves.

"Is that what you saw, saw?" asked a high-pitched voice, repeating the last word like a bird call.

"Yes, yes, I'm sure he's one," replied a deeper, rounder voice.

Cary craned his neck around in search of the voices.

"We just can't go plucking up any little thing like that without being sure, sure," said the higher voice.

"Sure?" replied the deeper voice, pressing its advantage. "How many bottom-feeders have you seen, seen these days as small as you, on the island, perched, perched in a tree? Chirrup! Exactly! Of course he's the one."

"Look, look. Now what have you done? He's heard us," scolded the higher voice.

"My fault is it, is it? I distinctly heard your twittering as well," the deeper voice retorted. "We must act, act immediately."

The conversation halted.

Cary searched the branches above him. Two birds dropped from their cover in a flurry of beating wings and alighted farther out on the branch on which he stood.

The two birds were half Cary's height, dark and speckled. Their eyes glared red and yellow.

"Hey," Cary said, "I've already been kidnapped by one bird. I'm not flying anywhere until someone—some bird tells me what's going on. What do you want?"

"Now what, what?" the bird with the lighter voiced asked.

"We have to take him," said the deeper-voiced bird. "Orders."

"What orders?" asked Cary. "What are you talking about? I was told to wait here, and that's what I'm doing."

"Let's to it, to it," said the lighter voiced bird, completely ignoring Cary.

"At once," agreed the one with the deeper voice.

"Aren't you listening?" asked Cary, his impatience seizing him, as if annoyed at Gregory. "I'm staying here."

The bird with the deeper voice lifted its head, warbled and clicked into the air.

"Did he send you?" Cary asked the birds, his confidence ebbing. "Do you understand what I'm saying?"

The branches around Cary filled with birds. Four more birds alighted on the branch in front of the arguing companions. Transfixed by the birds hopping toward him, Cary was unaware of the net hovering a few feet above his head. The net dropped. In a flap of wings Cary was knocked down, scooped up, net and all, and airlifted out of the tree into the morning sun.

Borne to a sudden height, Cary stopped struggling with the net lest the birds drop their troublesome cargo. He was suspended in the sky like a trapped insect hanging in the middle of a thick, hideous web. Dozens of birds, their sharp yellow beaks clamped on dozens of long tethers, were transporting him somewhere in a hurry.

The birds that had netted Cary were common starlings, a nuisance on the continent, but here his kidnappers were fleet-winged and daring, brandishing their sharp yellow beaks like weapons.

While he studied the birds, a thought struck him, as plain as the starlings' sharp beaks. He, along with his brother and sister, had shrunk.

It must have happened in the dining room, he thought, *in the fog.*

To what size, he could not be sure. He was at least twice the size of his spotted captors. Whether he had shrunk or the birds had grown, or a measure of both, his predicament was as obvious as his coarsely woven net; he could easily end up as someone's dinner.

The small murmuration of starlings broke into two groups and skilfully wove the tethers into two long braids. Not a tether out of place, the braids almost complete, the birds began abandoning the tethers. The starlings that remained could not bear Cary's weight. He was falling, fast.

As the features of the terrain rushed to meet him, Cary was thrown under shadow, as if overhead someone had opened an enormous black umbrella. Above him, two dark creatures, wings as broad as pterodactyls, had each clutched a braid of tethers in a single large talon. Vultures! Their distinctive collars, large, hooked beaks, and fuzzy pale heads were unmistakable. But these vultures were armoured with interlaced straps of dark leather.

The armour-clad giants bore Cary clumsily, tossing him back and forth like a doll in a shopping bag. Cary hung on to the net, closed his eyes and waited for the free-swinging pendulum to stop.

He thought about Gregory, how he had once trapped him under a blanket and carried him to his room, his little brother struggling in his arms, begging to be let go.

"The little pickpocket deserved it," Cary whispered, wondering again where the other birds had taken his brother and Clarisse.

When the vultures settled into soaring, Cary opened his eyes. Behind him were the last reaches of a pale and lifeless desert. A range of mountain peaks leapt away to his left, the same mountains he had seen when they first arrived, moments before the attack.

Cary surveyed the landscape. He wanted to remember features of the terrain in case of a later escape.

Past the last skirts of the mountains, the vultures glided down over a lush forest. A narrow river wound its way through the trees before it trailed out into broad, open meadows like a slender, glistening snake basking under the warm sun. An animal or two skittered under cover, but not one bird dotted the sky.

After passing over the last trees of the forest, the vultures came into view of the canopy of an enormous tree, a tree that belonged in a giant's orchard. It could have reached half way up the cliffs under the Giant's Table back home.

Impossible, Cary thought.

The vultures descended as they approached. A haphazard grove of long vines hung from beneath the trees' canopy like the tendrils of a jellyfish, which, reaching the nutrient-rich earth, had burrowed underground, borne roots and transformed from long, hanging vines into sturdy pillars bracing the wide canopy high above. In the middle, like a mother among its babies, rose the gargantuan trunk.

The expansive trunk was completely overlaid in vines as thick and round as the largest of the braces, wrapped around the trunk like a tangle of giant snakes. Not an inch of the trunk beneath was visible. The vine tower and the greatest number of braces stood atop two concentric base levels of rock. The trunk's base was a cascade of mountainous roots that bounded over and through splits in the rock, diving into the surrounding earth. The tree tower was enthroned on the brink of a cliff that fell from a breathless height to the foaming sea.

A perfect home for an army of birds, thought Cary.

With a short skid and a bump, Cary's captors clumsily landed him outside the root tower in front of a large, dark portal leading into the trunk. The two vultures folded in their wings and stood like dark-feathered dinosaurs on either side of him. Two large seagulls tottered out of the darkness, each decorated with a garland around its neck.

"This is one," croaked one of the vultures.

Cary was standing in the middle of the collapsed net. The larger of the two gulls dipped its head and inspected him with an unfeeling eye.

"You know the law," the larger gull said.

"Yes, yes," replied the vulture, not in the least intimidated by the gull. "As well as you. Is he here?"

"Yes."

The other vulture that had helped transport Cary had craned its hooked beak up to the higher dark portals in the tower. Curious birds had begun to pop into every hook and hollow. The vulture tossed his head toward the gathering audience, which caught the attention of the gull in charge.

"The Bottom-feeder must be presented to Harfan," said the gull. "Take it inside. Council will decide."

The vulture that had spoken first motioned with a toss of its head for Cary to follow the gulls inside.

"Not through here," grated one gull. "Through the stronghold. Let the assembly get a gander at it."

The vultures marshalled another flock of birds that airlifted Cary, like a crane hoists a shipping net, straight up to the canopy. The transport passed through the branches to the centre of the tree. Incredibly, though the vines that formed the perimeter of the trunk were several paces thick, its centre was hollow, like a dark, empty well, as if the original trunk had rotted or been eaten away, and all that remained were the giant, strangling vines.

Cary's transport hovered over the wide, dark hole. Cary thought for a moment he might be dropped, but the birds were only aligning their position before their descent.

As many tangled, grey-barked giant vines lined the inside as out, but inside, every cleft and cavity was crowded with birds, hundreds of them, of every colour and size.

No wonder I didn't see many birds, thought Cary. They're all in here.

Two large statues of birds, standing side by side, emerged out of the dull gloom, their heads tilted up as if

scorning mountain peaks far away. The faces of the sculpted birds were strong and proud. Their outside wings were
fanned up and out in a large display of pointed primary
feathers, a slender sword among the primaries. The inside wings curved down to form a flat, broad seat where a
large bird could perch comfortably; it was a magnificent
throne.

The birds lowered Cary to the uneven stone floor. After he freed himself from the net, he raised his head to the
round plate of sky high above him. The round unblinking
eyes of a thousand birds dotted the snaking roots of the
towering hollow.

It's me, Cary thought, averting his eyes. *They're staring
at me as if I were a cat.*

CHAPTER FOUR

Huʃgard

"What's happening?" Clarisse asked breathlessly as she watched her brothers carried off in different directions.

"We have passed through the Veil," answered the bird under Clarisse. "You have come to Shelter Island over enemy territory. We are being attacked."

"Attacked! Why? Where's your leader taking Cary, and where is Gregory?"

"Do not worry about your brothers. Of us three, Vaskar is the strongest and Ofost is the fastest," said the bird in between breaths. "I have yet to see a bird that can catch her. I am Gren, or else called the Feathered Fox. I may not fly as fast as Ofost, but even she will admit, I can be clever."

Clarisse's escort climbed toward a large cluster of clouds, piled high like a lopsided stack of cotton balls, a perfect place to hide. Far below, four or five black dots were chasing a larger one, the golden-armoured bird bearing Cary. Closer, two other birds were racing after her and her escort. A shriek stabbed the sky.

Stroke by stroke their assailants closed the gap as she and her escort shot into the clouds.

Clarisse was suddenly pulled in every direction. It was as if she were on a wild rocking horse that not only rocked forward and back, but side to side as well. The feathers on the back of her escort's head flashed in and out of view as it darted through the white mist.

"Are your feet in the stirrups?" asked Gren.

"Yes," answered Clarisse.

"Lean forward. Reach as far down as you can on the straps."

Clarisse obeyed.

"Good, we are going to climb again."

Clarisse clung on and closed her eyes. She resisted the pull to fall back as Gren made a steep ascent. When she felt level again, Clarisse opened her eyes. The white wisps of cloud sailed far below.

"While those rascals are searching the clouds," Gren said, "we will fly to the next."

Clarisse could never have imagined flying so high. In Freeton, or anywhere else on the Fragile Lands, there were so few planes that only officials in the government got the chance to fly over the continent. Her parents had once taken her to the top of the Giant's Table, an escarpment so high that Clarisse imagined jumping on the pillowy clouds drifting below, but the height to which Gren had ascended made her dizzy by comparison.

"Brace yourself," said Gren, breaking Clarisse's thoughts. "Now we must dive."

Clarisse stretched her arms down the strap harness, burying her face in Gren's soft-feathered neck. She closed her eyes and sucked in a last breath before the plunge. The racing wind grew to a roar, its steady stream pouring over her head as if she were standing under a waterfall.

When the pulses stopped and Clarisse opened her eyes, Gren was flying in the swirling white mists of another cloud. But their safe haven was smaller than the last, and in a few wing strokes, the puffy white breaths melted away. They flew for the next cloud, and the next, until, some miles from their assailants, Gren glided down over a mountain range.

Now I'm sure we're not at home, Clarisse thought. A long line of mountains stretching to both horizons does not exist anywhere on the Fragile Lands.

The fugitives flew on low through the mountains, weaving from peak to peak until they approached three mountains that were higher than the others.

"We must avoid the Vulton Crags and Soltin Myrr," said Gren. "Our enemies, the Vultori, guard those crags. The bog is an enemy to all creatures."

"Where?" asked Clarisse.

"Ahead of you," answered her escort. "On your right."

A large grey ridge floated above the haze, and below its cliffs, a dark void blotted the landscape.

What a strange island this is, Clarisse thought. *Why has no one from Freeton ever mentioned it, especially our parents?* She concluded that the govenor must have been keeping it a secret.

Gren banked left and headed out over a wide, barren landscape. When they reached the coastline they turned north and followed the shore. Safely out of range of the Vulton Crags, Gren soared into a wide turn and headed back to the mountains. But with all his climbing and diving, and the added miles, Clarisse's escort had finally begun to tire. If Gren had to evade another assault, he would not be able to outfly his attackers.

Once through the mountain range, an enormous golden carpet rolled ahead into the horizon. Her escort swooped down and skimmed over the rolling waves of long yellow grass. Clarisse thought correctly that Gren, the Feathered Fox, was camouflaging his golden-fringed feathers against the field.

By this time, the responsibilities of home had been lost in the adventure of Clarisse's escape. Her eyes were full of the sights and sounds of her new surroundings, as if she had flown into the pages of a favourite book, but one she had never read.

Gren banked to his left to follow a river. The sweeping golden sea rolled away on their right, and a lush forest of old trees guarded the river on her left.

"This is the Freewind, which winds through the southern reaches of Arafen," said Gren, anticipating her questions. "There are friendly eyes upon us."

Out of one wood, through another, they flew on.

Finally, after weaving through the trunks of taller trees in a deeper wood, the weary bird approached the base of a high cliff, a towering wall of rock strewn with long leafy vines, which hung like garlands on its craggy grey face. Free from the last trees, Gren headed straight for the stone wall. Clarisse thought the bird was going to fly straight into the rock, but just above the level of the forest canopy, camouflaged by hanging overgrown vines, was the mouth of a cave. Gren alighted on its lip and hopped from tooth to tooth toward the dark throat. Armoured like Gren, birds stood like solemn statues on either side, watching from the shadows. Two more hops and Clarisse was suddenly in flight again inside a large underground cavern.

Though a distance beyond the cavern's mouth, everything around her remained visible. Where was the source of the strange light painting her arms and her escort's feathers with a warm glow? Golden veins, similar in colour to Gren's golden-feathered mail, intermingled across the cavern walls like branches growing in intricate patterns. Every branch of gold shone as if it were a thin, sparkling brook, as though from the top of the cavern, molten gold was running down the sides of the stone walls in hundreds of thin, spidery rivulets. It gave the otherwise cold and damp cave a warm and comfortable feeling.

Ahead, strange cones hung from the ceiling like cream-coloured icicles inlaid with glowing golden veins. Directly beneath the icicles were cones of all different sizes. Some icicles and cones had joined and formed large columns. Her science teacher loved to draw illustrations on the board. Clarisse had sketched her own illustration of a cavern. The cones above were stalactites, stalagmites below, but she had never seen anything like these.

Clarisse and her escort wove through the columns, rising and falling, until at last Gren swept up on fully opened wings and alighted on a raised dais of smooth stone.

With Clarisse perched comfortably on his shoulders, the bird piped out a complex string of soft chips and tweets, which sounded a bit like Morse code. A moment later, a soft murmur of similar sounds filled the cavern as bird after bird hopped from the shadows, but not only birds but also squirrels, foxes and other animals.

"So the report is true," said a voice from among the throng of animals. "You were attacked, as we had feared.

Where is Vaskar?"

Clarisse dismounted. She watched an owl three times her height step from the shadow onto the large, polished stone mantle. It was a barn owl. She had seen the creatures several times at a local bird sanctuary. It had sparked her interest, and she had posted pictures on the wall of her bedroom. But with the owl so close, its mysterious dark eyes and its curled black talons peeking from under its feathers, Clarisse would measure her words and keep her distance.

Many of the creatures cocked their heads. Beaks and snouts bobbed back and forth between her and the owl as if they were waiting for some spectacle to unfold. A chipmunk, its whiskers dancing with curiosity, hopped closer.

Clarisse backed away from its long incisors. *It's half my size*, she thought.

"He ordered us away. Ofost rolled to the left, I to the right. After that I lost contact," said Gren, as if reporting to someone in command.

"Gregory and I are here, safe," said Ofost. "Greetings, Gren."

Gregory ran to Clarisse, nearly knocking her over in a tackle of a hug.

"I had no doubt," Gren added. "No winged creature is faster, north or south of the Golden Fields."

"By all accounts," began the owl again, "the report we have heard is true. Vaskar has fallen."

"Fallen?" erupted Gren, Clarisse looking on anxiously. "How?"

A young bird timidly moved forward.

"I saw him," he said. "Or I think I saw him. I was chasing my sister through the branches of a tree when I heard birdfolc—fighting. I flew to the end of the branch. That's when I saw them."

"Saw whom?" said Gren with some impatience.

"Gildenhyrn Gren, the bird is young. Patience," said the owl, turning his gaze to the young bird. "This young warrior, a descendant of our Folc, has passed over much of Shelter Island, flying below a Gildenhyrn sent to rescue you, at some danger to himself, I might add. I once flew side by side with a young bird like that."

Gren dipped his beak toward his talons, an offer of respect and trust among the Gildenhyrn warriors, who seldom lowered a watchful eye. He urged the young bird to continue, which had the effect of making him more courageous in his delivery of the account of Vaskar's fall.

"Gildenhorn Baskar, I mean Vaskar ... Gilden-hyrn ... and the others were fighting—yes, fighting," said the young bird.

"How many others?" Ofost asked.

The young bird splayed his short primary feathers and started to count. "Two, three, four, five, yes five—no, six others," answered the fledgling, "all taking turns—one, then another—attacking him. There were too many. He fell—not fell, exactly, but..."

The young one spread its wings and acted out a spiralling descent. Nearing the end of the demonstration, it stopped, unsure whether to continue. A flick of the owl's primary feathers motioned for the bird to continue.

"The other birds followed Vaskar—to the ground," the young bird continued, "and called others. There were too many. Vaskar was wounded. The other birds covered him with a net and took him."

"What of the young man?" asked Gren. "Did you see

an Earth-dweller?"

"No, I didn't see an Earth-dweller—what is a jung man?" the young one asked the owl. "Can I go back now?"

The owl nodded his consent. The young bird hopped back to his Gildenhyrn friend and escort that had brought him.

"I have failed. I have failed the three. I have failed the Gildenhyrn," said Gren.

He bowed his head, his wings spread forward, revealing a bright sword from among the primary wing feathers of each wing.

"I surrender the swords of my order," he continued, to Clarisse's astonishment.

"Nonsense!" said the owl, brushing up Gren's wings with a sweep of his large wing. "This is not the time for any one of us to be surrendering anything. Our enemies have taken Vaskar, and in all likelihood the boy. I refuse your request. Keep your swords. You have not failed anyone. You have courageously followed orders, and with the help of Ofost, you have brought two of our Ascentors safely to Husgard."

The owl raised his voice, "You may continue your commission in the Gildenhyrn by escorting your charge to her chamber. As for all other folc here attending, you are dismissed."

Gren approached Clarisse.

"Why did the owl call us 'Ascentors'?" asked Clarisse, with Gregory tagging along at her side, his wide eyes trying to take in the new sights and sounds all at once.

"You are in the Song," answered Gren, "the Song of Fridorfold. The owl, as you call him, is Mandwar, Guardian of Husgard Hellir."

As the golden-armoured bird walked ahead of her and Gregory, he recited similar words to those she had first read from the pouch.

> "*Three golden feathers found and freed,*
> *Three golden-winged bearers to bear the three*
> *Three feather's bearers, then shall lead*
> *On wings born of Fridorfold*
> *As Ascentors three."*

"But what's an Ascentor?" asked Clarisse, who was now very tired. She hoped she had not sounded rude repeating the question.

As her escort walked under an archway, he cocked his head back. "You are now like Mandwar," Gren said, "a Guardian ... a leader."

Clarisse stopped. "Leader?" she said aloud. "Leader of what?"

"A queen!" put in Gregory.

"Leader of whom and of what shall be made clear when the moon has fled," replied her escort as he rounded a corner.

CHAPTER FIVE
The Reckoning

In the overcrowded, eerie silence, every round penetrating eye fixed upon him, Cary remained mute. Six large birds, including the two decorated gulls Cary had already met, hobbled out from the shadows. The sextet of gulls separated and shuffled over to either side of the bird throne, three to a side, wing to wing. The grey-white males and mottled brown females fixed their hungry, cold eyes upon him. Cary stiffened.

A murmur arose from the myriad birds that crowded the tower as another large bird ambled out, older, its collar feathers greying, though not decorated like the gulls'. All fell silent.

The large old bird, a crow or possibly a raven, crossed the stone shelf and stood behind Cary. It greeted no one. All through the assembly heads turned, each to its neighbour. The host of birds had expected their leader to take the High Seat, as he had always done.

"A Earth-dweller stands before you," the large greying bird said in a steady tone.

The leader leaned down to Cary. "Turn around."

"What?" Cary answered, thinking he would be struck.

"Turn around and lift your raiment."

"My what?"

"Turn around," repeated the bird, unfolding a wing.

Cary turned his back to the assembly.

The old grey bird brushed a wing tip up Cary's back and lifted his shirt. "You know the law. An Earth-dweller"—the old bird swung its beak to the contemptuous gulls"—has come to the island. He bears the mark. What have you to say?"

The old bird released Cary's shirt.

The murmuring among the birds burst forth again, quickly rising to a clamour of bird tweets and chatter.

The old grey bird cocked his head and surveyed the root tower. Returning his gaze to the middle, he trumpeted a loud and defiant caw, silencing the noisy assembly as if he had snatched their tongues.

"What do you say?" he asked into the hush, a question that sounded like a command.

One lone voice broke the silence and piped out, "Ascentor." Others joined in. "Ascentor! Ascentor!" cried the chorus.

"You have spoken it," pronounced the old bird. "As the sign dictates, as the law decrees, Ascentor he shall be."

The puzzled gulls on either side of their grey leader swung their agape beaks to each other, as if long-laid plans had been swept away in an instant. Two smaller birds with hooked beaks, bearing themselves like guards, hopped up to the platform and stood in front of the High Seat.

"Follow me," ordered the grey bird as it walked off the

platform toward a darkened archway.

Two gulls that had been standing on either side of the throne tottered on webbed feet over to Cary.

"Follow," one said, nudging Cary along with a firm push of his wing. Between two stern gulls, tucking in his shirt as he went, he left the towering hall the same way the old grey bird had departed.

Leaving the two gulls behind, Cary entered a large chamber carved out of a natural hollow in the tangle of giant roots that formed the tower's wall. A large round porthole leading to the outside world supplied a brighter light. The old bird was conferring in a low voice with a smaller, mail-clad bird. Observing that Cary had come in, the two birds ended their discussion and turned toward him.

"I apologize for the manner—the way in which you have been unceremoniously transported to Vangorfold, our home," said the large greying bird haltingly, possibly to choose his words carefully or because he was old, "but the matter before us was—urgent. You have been appointed as an Ascentor, and an Ascentor you shall be. You have come to us in perilous times, but not untimely."

The mail-clad bird flew out.

"I've been kidnapped. My sister and brother are missing, and I have no idea where I am." Cary paused. "And I'm hungry. I don't even know what an Ascentor is. What if I don't want to be an Ascentor?"

The grave old bird spoke to a servant and returned his attention to Cary.

"You are now our Ascentor, a position of leadership reserved for a Earth-dweller. It means you shall both lead and judge—not without guidance, of course. The choice is not yours. You bear the mark; you have been named."

"What mark?" Cary asked.

"The token of our folc, on your back."

Cary lifted his shirt and thrust his chin over his shoulder. His back and the mark stubbornly remained hidden.

"Wings," offered the old bird, his head cocked to the side, fascinated at Cary's attempt to find the proof. "in faint threads on your back."

Cary gave up, not wanting to look like a dog chasing its tail. The six large birds that had been standing beside the throne entered the chamber. Four were seagulls, male and female birds twice Cary's height, their eyes glittering like round black jewels, unflinching and fearless. The menacing crew formed a half-circle behind him.

Cary had always regarded gulls as rather harmless and stupid, comical even, but their imposing presence compared with his shrunken self was unnerving.

He wondered what had happened to the golden mail-clad bird, the heroic-looking warrior that had left him in the tree. Cary recalled his sister and brother, straddled over the shoulders of the other birds. Why hadn't their escorts flown Clarisse and Gregory to the tree tower, to Vangorfold?

With a turn of the old one's head, the birds that had followed Cary into the chamber were dismissed. The hurried servant bird replaced them through another entrance. He laid before Cary a tray of food, which consisted mainly of nuts but also held fruit and small flat biscuits, even some water in a small bowl. While Cary sated his appetite, the old grey bird stood in front of the large round porthole that served as both window and door and studied the sky.

As Cary finished his meal, a raptor landed on the sill

of the porthole facing the grey bird. It was wearing scaled armour over its breast, possibly interlaced fish scales, not at all like the feathered golden mail of the birds that had flown out of the fog. When Cary lowered his drinking bowl, a thin membrane skimmed over the raptor's eye, which fixed on Cary. It leaned forward and whispered to the old crow.

Having delivered its message the fierce warrior cocked a suspicious eye toward Cary, then darted off.

"I apologize again for the rough treatment you have endured," said the old crow, turning. "As a leader, you will soon discover ... one cannot always ensure details of orders will be strictly followed. I am sorry I could not introduce myself before now. My name is Harfan." He offered a short bow of his head. "Your name, I believe, is Cary."

Cary wiped his mouth with a woven piece of material that had been provided with the meal and nodded.

Harfan continued, "I understand you have a brother and sister."

"Clarisse," answered Cary, "and Gregory. We were attacked by some birds."

Harfan returned to the porthole window. "That was unfortunate. Nevertheless, you are safe. I have my best scouts searching as we speak. Their captain has delivered a message."

"What did he say?" asked Cary, who had grown more comfortable in the presence of the old bird.

Harfan paused. "Your brother and sister have been captured by rebels, your enemies."

"Captured?" asked Cary, remembering how the golden mail-clad raptors had compelled them to leave. "My enemies?"

49

"They will not likely be ill-treated. We will find your brother and sister. But we have more pressing matters before us. You have been elevated to Ascentor; I serve, at present, as Harfan, your Steward. As Steward of Vangorfold and Advisor, I will be counselling you in all matters regarding the island, till such time"—the old grey bird paused longer than usual—"until you grow more familiar with our ways."

"What am I supposed to do?" asked Cary.

"Assist in governing our island."

Cary fell silent. He liked the sound of that, being a leader, a real leader of a real realm, even if it was over gulls and other birds on some forgotten island.

"Your first duty," continued Harfan, "is at hand. Today is Folclaguhaus, our day of court. Birdfolc, our people, as you might say, have come together for trying alleged ... injustices, as Earth-dwellers would say. You must take the High Seat to judge on all matters brought before you. Ten cases, I believe, today."

"Today?" Cary objected. "I don't know your laws."

"I will be at your side to inform you of all you need to know. Each case will be presented ... attended by witnesses. You need only weigh the evidence. You decide guilt or innocence according to our laws, laws which are read aloud before each case. The cases are of ... minor consequence."

Cary imagined himself seated on the magnificently sculpted High Seat. "When does it start?" he asked.

"Commencement of Folclaguhaus has passed," answered the Steward, who had extended a wing toward the passageway Cary had passed through not half an hour before.

Cary got up, brushed a few crumbs from his clothes, and walked the passageway leading to the main hall and the High Seat.

When he came into the hall, the murmur hushed. The birds had been waiting for Harfan and Cary to rejoin the assembly. Cary approached the High Seat and stopped. He turned to Harfan, uncertain about what to do. Harfan unfolded a wing and gently pressed Cary toward the High Seat.

The old bird pointed its unfurled wing toward Cary. "Here stands your Ascentor."

One of the mottled brown gulls who had taken her former position behind the High Seat with the others approached Cary. She laid a cape of woven fabric over Cary's shoulders. Its texture reminded Cary of the soft weave of a swallow's nest.

As soon as the cape had been laid across Cary's shoulders, every bird present extended a wing toward the High Seat. Cary interpreted the gesture as an invitation and took his position in front of the sculpted birds that formed the seat. He was about to hoist himself up onto the seat when he was interrupted by the Steward.

"Do you pledge to abide by the laws, decrees and traditions of Vangorfold, to discharge with honour the responsibilities of Ascentor?"

Cary thought of the only words people used on solemn occasions at home and said, "I do."

Two gulls shuffled to Cary's side. The two officials fanned a wing behind him, scooped him up and placed him on the High Seat. As soon as Cary touched the seat, the arena burst into a deafening cacophony of bird calls.

Once more, Harfan silenced the gathering of Birdfolc.

The steward briefly reminded all in attendance of the seriousness of the day. Satisfied with the assembly's silent anticipation, he asked that the first bird be brought forward for his day of justice.

Cary listened intently as a bird described the case before him. The bird in question had been caught red-handed—or with its claw in the cradle, as it was put, stealing food from stores set aside for the guards and leaders of Vangorfold Stronghold, the very tower in which the assembly had gathered. The witnesses made statements and produced evidence found in the accused's quarters.

The accused bird held his head low, possibly because he was ashamed or perhaps to brace himself for the Ascentor's judgement. Seeing an opportunity, and breaking a long standing tradition at Folclaguhaus, Cary addressed the accused bird directly.

"Did you take these things without permission?"

The accused raised its beak in the direction of Harfan. The old grey bird stood as still as the statues carved on the throne. Harfan would not interfere. The puzzled prisoner lowered its beak to the stone floor.

"Ascentor—I stole the food," the bird answered, "twice."

The bird had confessed to the second offence without any evidence against him.

Believing the confession had moved Cary, Harfan approached the High Seat.

"As Ascentor you must only decide guilt or innocence. Your councillors will decide upon and declare his punishment."

The greying Steward moved aside, but not as far from Cary as he had been at first. He had not been given the words for declaring a judgement. After a moment, he remembered the words spoken by a judge over a radio broadcast.

"I pronounce you guilty as charged."

Unlike the courts of the Fragile Lands, which enforced silence throughout proceedings, the Birdfolc whooped, hooted and cawed, not only because the accused bird had justly been found guilty, but because the act of addressing the accused directly, an entirely new practice, should rightly fall to the Ascentor. Cary was pleased.

He gained confidence over the next three cases (all to do with stealing), and for the fifth case heard a straightforward matter involving territory and trees, which was followed by a more complicated case in which a pair of larger birds had intimidated a smaller bird into paying for protection, the payment made in the form of collected nest-building materials and food. Cary had followed a blackmail case in the newspapers on the Fragile Lands, which helped him understand the crime. Many Birdfolc had attended Folclaguhaus as supporting witnesses. The day drew to a close with a case dealing with the rightful heirs to a tree.

Although Cary was feeling more confident, the events of the day—listening carefully to so many witnesses, weighing testimony, and deciding guilt or innocence—had unexpectedly exhausted him.

Punishments ranged from publicly pulling out tail feathers of thieves (the Steward had assured Cary the feathers were of the sort that grew back within a month or two) to forced restitution or "cage time" for more serious crimes, such as forcing a bird to abandon her nest.

By now, the great crowd of birds had quieted, possibly as weary as Cary from the day-long proceedings. Harfan was consulting with one of the gulls.

Finally, he approached Cary. "One case remains ... a matter concerning treason."

Cary motioned for Harfan to draw closer. "Can't we hear it tomorrow?" he asked in a low voice.

"Today is Folclaguhaus, the day of court," admonished the Steward. "You must hear all cases brought before you this day. The next Folclaguhaus is many turns of the earth from now. The last case before you concerns the security of Vangorfold."

Without waiting for a reply, the Steward motioned for the last case to be brought forward.

CHAPTER SIX
Crime and Punishment

Gren led Clarisse and Gregory to an inner chamber, its walls interlaced with golden branches that radiated a warm light. Clarisse immediately fixed her eyes upon a large round bed, a mossy nest set on a raised platform of rock. The bed pulled at her exhausted limbs. Gregory ran over to the nest-bed and climbed in as though it were the best of treehouses. Gren watched Clarisse as she stood transfixed, staring at the bed, where Gregory had already made himself comfortable. As Gren started to back out of the chamber, Clarisse stopped him.

"Gren," said Clarisse. "My parents ... we have to go back."

"Ascentor Arithi, when you passed into our world on the wings of the Gildenhyrn, you passed into times passing."

"Times passing?" asked Clarisse. "And why did you call me Arithi?"

"Please," answered Gren, "if you wish it, I will answer your questions and tell you much of what has been and has come to pass in our world."

Anxious to learn as much as she could about this new strange world, Clarisse reclined on the large round nest, propping herself up on the rim with a cushion. Gregory, refreshed from his nap on the back of Ofost, was ready and willing to stay up all night.

Gren settled onto an elevated beam, designed to be gripped by talons. He had taken off his helmet but still wore the light gold mail armour. He was no ordinary bird, but a raptor, a warrior.

He began. "In times passing and times past, past countless turns of the earth, when Birdfolc and Earth-dwellers spoke a common tongue, the land and all who lived upon it were at peace, bound by oaths to be stewards of earth and sky. Earth-dwellers tilled the soil, fished the seas and watched the skies. Likewise, Birdfolc watched the skies but also soared beyond the slow turns of the earth, interpreting signs, reading the sea, the stars, the sun and the moon. Times passed under one united realm. The Fragile Lands was Fridorfold, a realm of peace, united in our Song."

"What happened?" asked Clarisse eagerly.

"Pledges were broken; our peace was torn," answered Gren.

"How?" asked Clarisse.

Gren's dark pupil traced the golden streams on the chamber's wall as if following a long, winding memory. "War," he answered. "War and deceit."

"Between the birds and us?" asked Clarisse. "I mean, the people—the Earth-dwellers and Birdfolc?"

"Not at the beginning," answered Gren. "Birdfolc first fought Birdfolc. Strong leaders arose from our folc and began to debate the signs, arguing our time with Earth-dwellers, the destroyers of the earth, had finished, that the realm of Fridorfold had ended, that Birdfolc must free and heal what remained of the earth. Others argued the signs pointed to the renewing of our pledge with Earth-dwellers as stewards, to continue in the Song. Our leaders debated our path over many turns of the earth.

"Many of our folc, persuaded we must continue apart, shunned Earth-dwellers. Earth-dwellers soon learned of the division among us. Out of pride, or from impatience, many Earth-dwellers dismissed us as dreamers and deceivers and refused to communicate with any winged creature. It was into that time passing Raven Wisefaest, a servant of the Ellri, conspired with an ambitious Earth-dweller, Faesten Sax, to drive a wedge between our folc and Earth-dwellers."

"How?" asked Clarisse.

"By doing the unthinkable," answered Gren. "Wisefaest secretly robbed Birdfolc of many of their eggs. He arranged for the stolen eggs to be transported to Faesten Sax, alias Knife, who, in turn, sold our heirs to Earth-dwellers—to eat. For his crime, the raven has since been named Blodcroew.

"After some turns of the earth, Blodcroew claimed that he had found the criminal responsible, that he had tracked down a flying beast in the form of a snake, which, when it was young, had slipped into our nests under shadow. Blodcroew flew to meet this serpent in battle and destroyed it, or so he said. His victory over the serpent secured his leadership, winning the hearts of many of our folc.

"Blodcroew and his council passed laws that forbade

our folc to communicate with Earth-dwellers. Over many turns of the earth, suspecting the Birdfolc were planning an attack, Earth-dwellers began to hunt us. Our folc were forced to find refuge in the highest trees, unreachable cliffs and remote places of the continent you now call the Fragile Lands. It had been Blodcrow's aim all along to drive a wedge between Birdfolc and Earth-dwellers and destroy the hope and song of Fridorfold.

"Through times passing, our shared language was forgotten. Only a small number of Earth-dwellers could speak with our folc, and likewise, our folc with Earth-dwellers. There have been many turns of the earth and times passing since."

Gregory, happy to stay up well past his bedtime, had been trying to follow the story but had finally given into the comfortable downy pillows and fallen asleep. A woven tapestry of strange birds in various places had captivated Clarisse, each picture playing a part in a larger story.

Gren braced his talons. "But you are tired. We will finish the story tomorrow."

"No, no, continue. Please." Though tired, as Gren had observed, Clarisse had been thinking about how Blodcroew had gotten his name.

"The bird on the tapestry with his wings out of shape, the one that looks like he's falling. Who is that?"

"That," said Gren, "is Blodcroew."

"Why is he falling? Did someone fight him?"

Gren, convinced Clarisse had been closely following his story, continued.

"Blodcroew's crime of robbing Birdfolc of their young, to be eaten like common chickens, was what Earth-dwellers call murder. Blodcroew is falling because he was cast out of the Realm of Ellri for his evil conspiracy. He made Earth-dwellers a stench to Birdfolc. He was no longer a singer, but a sorcerer."

"How was he caught?" asked Clarisse, who had been waiting patiently for Gren to come to this part of the story.

"Ascentor Arithi, your namesake, now joins the story." Clarisse's eyebrows arched. Gren's statement had had its intended effect.

"I will continue and all will be made clear," said Gren. "After Blodcroew accused Wyrm of eating eggs and swallowing others to deliver to Knife, the raven defeated the serpent in a flying battle, as it was reported. None but a few of Blodcroew's cronies actually witnessed the battle. Wyrm, it was said, fell dead to the earth. Many Earth-dwellers went to the place to see what great thing had fallen from the sky in smoke and ruin. Among the curious was a young Earth-dweller, no older than you."

Clarisse was wondering why there were no records of these events in the Freeton Library.

"But there was not much to see, only charred trees standing like thin dark spectres within a smoking, black circle of earth. There was no trace of the flying serpent, so folc and Earth-dwellers returned without a story—all but three: Knife, Blodcroew and your namesake, the young Arithi."

"Thinking everyone had left, Knife openly accused Blodcroew of using him for his own ends. He asked, now that Wyrm had been destroyed, how the raven was going to continue delivering eggs.

"Blodcroew was one step ahead. The raven needed to dispose of outspoken rebels and promised to deliver

Birdfolc to Knife to hoard as slaves, under one condition. Knife would never contact him again. Knife had planned to hatch some of the eggs to grow his captive population. Blodcroew's proposition would, in time, produce more eggs, which meant more gold, so Knife accepted. Blodcroew spread his wings, threatened Knife with the same fate of Wyrm if he broke his word, and flew off. Not understanding what she had heard, young Arithi—"

"The name you called me," interrupted Clarisse.

"You will understand why as the story of this time past draws to an end."

Gren continued, "Young Arithi ran home. She kept what she had heard a secret. Through many turns of the earth, Arithi the Brave secretly discovered where Knife set up his cages. Blodcroew kept his promise. He delivered Birdfolc to Knife, prisoners Blodcroew had exiled for treason under his new laws, to suffer as egg-bearing slaves, or suffer the axe. Knife has earned his name.

"One night, when Knife was away selling his eggs, Arithi freed the captive Birdfolc. The birds had been tagged and had flight-feathers pulled, so they could not fly, so Arithi led her new friends to a secret hollow that she had prepared near her home. As exiles of Fridorfold and slaves of Knife, the freed Birdfolc had nowhere to go. Arithi assisted in relaying messages, carried by animals the Birdfolc trusted, messages which, in some turns of the earth, found the ears of Mandwar."

"Mandwar?" wondered Clarisse. "That's the name of the owl you were talking with."

"The same."

"The same? He would be ages old by now."

"He is old," replied Gren. "He has been given many

times as a Guardian of Fridorfold. He has lived through many times passing. In fact, you passed into our time when you were transported to Shelter Island and to Husgard."

"I don't understand," said Clarisse, trying to visualize times intersecting other times.

"You have on Earth what you call a gyroscope?"

"Yes, it's a toy with orbiting rings spinning around each other at different speeds."

"Times passing is similar. On Shelter Island time passes much slower than in the Fragile Lands. From the Realm of Ellri, another ring if you like, one may see all things, what is happening on the Fragile Lands as well as on Shelter Island. Those with the gift—like Aevi—can see into the third ring of times passing, thus seeing many things."

Gren paused. "Mandwar will explain it better."

"Who is Aevi?" Clarisse asked, trying to commit all these new names to memory.

"Aevi? Aevi is your brother, Gregory," answered Gren. "Mandwar believes that he has the gift and will test him under the Dome of Times Passing. That too, you will see."

Overwhelmed by so many new revelations, Clarisse could only sit on the edge of her round bed, blinking from Gregory to the tapestry on the nearest wall, recalling the scenes of Gren's story.

"Please, I will continue the story?" Gren asked.

"Yes," answered Clarisse, her mind on the images over the tapestry.

"When Mandwar received the messages, he sent out many loyal folc to confirm what he had heard. When the facts had been confirmed and the exiles delivered to him in secret, which is another story to be told, Mandwar and others confronted Blodcroew during Folclaguhaus, our day of justice. As expected, Blodcroew denied the charges and accused Mandwar and his followers of treason, as usurpers of his High Seat.

"To the surprise of the entire assembly, Mandwar presented Knife's former captives and Arithi to the court as witnesses, but their testimonies were never heard. Certain to be exposed, Blodcroew called for his guards, who flew to his aid, including many Blodcroew had appointed secretly, the order of fighters now loyal to Harfan—the Dreygar. However, Mandwar had predicted Blodcroew's attack. There was a battle.

"Birdfolc fled Folclaguhaus, except those loyal to Blodcroew or Mandwar. Outnumbered but more valiant, those loyal to Mandwar held off the attack, giving our Guardian the opportunity to carry Arithi to safety.

"As the Earth turned, Arithi's story spread. Many of our folc deserted Blodcroew and his lies and sought safe haven with Mandwar. At the next Folclaguhaus, Blodcroew was tried by the Ellri and sentenced for his crimes. Blodcroew was exiled but found refuge, it is said, somewhere beyond the seas where only a bird of his powers could survive. What you see pictured upon the tapestry is his fall.

"Meanwhile, Earth-dwellers grew in number and attacks on the Birdfolc mounted. Mandwar and those loyal to Fridorfold fled over the Fragile Lands to the ghost city of Draugon."

Clarisse had heard of Draugon, north of the Giant's Finger on the eastern side of the Fragile Lands. The city was deserted, on the other side of Oakenfen, which no one would pass. The forest held too many strange tales.

Gren continued, "If the Singers of Ellri had not intervened, we would have been destroyed, so they created Shelter Island and the Lost Veil to protect us, to make us invisible to the Fragile Lands."

"The Veil? You mean those storm clouds we passed through that came from nowhere?"

"Yes, from that time past, our folc have been hidden here, behind the Veil on Shelter Island. But even here Blodcroew's followers grew in number under Harfan. Our great tree was secretly poisoned. Harfan seized control. We fled to the caves of Husgard."

"Where is Blodcroew now?"

"None of our folc knows. I do not believe that he could have lived through so many times passing, as Mandwar has. But it is said that though Blodcroew had been cast out of the Realm of Ellri, he nevertheless possessed a measure of his former power."

"What happened to Arithi?"

"Arithi too has passed into time, yet her name has been honoured through many times. You are of her line, so named Arithi and Ascentor. You will help us restore Fridorfold."

Gren bowed his head.

"Arithi? I am not Arithi. I hardly know her story yet."

"Yet the name has been given to you. You have heard her story and now bear her name."

Clarisse was confused. *I'm Clarisse*, she thought. *The one who gives in to everybody. I'm Clarisse the Coward, not Arithi the Brave. What am I doing here?*

"Blodcroew is dead," Clarisse said, "or has passed into time. What use is the story now? What can I do?"

The memory of home rushed into her mind like beating wings. "I shouldn't even be here."

"Yet you are here, bearing the name of Arithi the Brave."

"But I'm not brave."

Gren had stood up, preparing to leave.

"And what about Gregory?"

"Aevi is safe here. He is under Mandwar's wing and teaching."

"Teaching?" asked Clarisse. "Teaching what?"

Gren had passed under the arch leading to the passageway. "How to use his gift," he answered. "But we have been long in the telling. I must take my leave."

Clarisse had hoped Gren's story would answer all her questions, but it had only created more. She lay back and cradled Gregory's head in her arm. She followed the golden branches that spread across her ceiling. She recalled Arithi, how brave she had been. She pictured Blodcroew and Mandwar and Shelter Island. Every golden branch led to another thought, another possibility, another scene in Gren's story. Clarisse followed the sparkling streams, now fading, into sleep.

CHAPTER SEVEN
Not Guilty

The bird summoned before the High Seat was unusual. Before Cary stood a bird he could not identify, half the size of the gulls. He had seen starlings, sparrows, pigeons, grosbeaks, chickadees, blue jays, finches of various colours, and birds of prey, but none like the bird standing before him. Its colours quivered like water, its feathers subtly alternating from shades of blue to turquoise, from turquoise to green with golden threads. Unlike the worried birds he had previously judged that day and the stern gulls, the bird held captive before Cary was composed, thoughtful. *I wonder what case they have against him?*

Harfan interrupted his thoughts. "Before the Ascentor is one Adarel, more commonly known as the Changeling."

When Harfan mentioned the title Ascentor, Cary caught the Changeling's eye. Not a drop of anger or fear stained its gaze. The prisoner bowed to Cary.

Harfan continued, "The Changeling has been—among others—allegedly leading a rebellion against Vangorfold, hence the charge of treason." Harfan paused. "Summon the witnesses."

Three witnesses entered the floor area. One was the fiercely clad raptor that had alighted on the sill of the porthole window. Another bird, a small, dark bird with a limp, followed behind, averting his eyes. The last to enter was a huge awkward vulture that towered over every bird present. Oddly, the wrinkle headed bird of prey was the most nervous, its eyes continually darting from the council to the crowd and back to Cary, as if it were on trial.

The steady raptor identified himself as Grimmar of the Dreygar. He described how the insurgency at Husgard was primarily formed around two individuals: Mandwar, called Stinga the Backstabber in Vangorfold, and the bird presently before the court, Adarel, the Changeling.

The small bird identified himself as Scrim. Cary understood him to be some sort of spy answerable only to Harfan. Scrim testified that he had seen the Changeling and Stinga conferring together on several occasions before the arranged exchange, unquestionably placing the two rebels in each other's confidence.

The Vulture, stammering and repeatedly clearing its snake-like throat, reported how the Changeling had been spotted more than once secretly recruiting Birdfolc under the cover of Vangorfen, to which there were many witnesses. One fact had been made clear: the Changeling was undoubtedly a captive leader of the rebellion.

Cary consulted with Harfan, who advised that if it were true, and it could be simply established the Changeling was one of the leaders of the rebellion, even by regular association, he would automatically be guilty of treason to Vangorfold, since the rebellion had already been officially condemned as treasonous.

As Cary continued in his conference with Harfan, every bird of the council spread open a wing and brandished a long grey sword. Two gulls, wings agape, sprang from behind to defend Harfan and Cary.

Standing on its hind legs, close enough to the Changeling to brush against its feathers, was a large rat. The guard who had been standing beside the Changeling was held prone under one of the rat's long feet. The lithe rat sported a long grin, as if it were at a picnic. He adroitly held the tip of one thin sword under the guard's beak beneath his foot while waving a second as a threat to any bird that foolishly chose to come too close.

The rat broke the silence. "Ascentor, before you stands no traitor. This is Adarel, a Singer of Ellri." A murmur rippled through the court. The rat turned to address the arena of Birdfolc. "He is not guilty of this charge. It is old Scarecrow who is guilty of treason, treason to Fridorfold."

The rat swung his long snout toward the guard edging toward him. "As light-footed as a galloping horse!" He crouched and sprang off into the near darkness at the back of the court. The Folclaguhaus assembly erupted into a cacophony of bird chatter.

Harfan had the council resume former positions and raised a wing to silence the spectators.

"The court has seen and heard the only defence of the Changeling—from a rat!"

Chirps and titters rose from the surrounding tower. Harfan quickly approached Cary.

"Who is old Scarecrow?" Cary asked.

"An affectionate name bestowed upon me by the rat and his companions," answered Harfan. "But we are not here today to discuss the various names I have been given by our enemies. We are here to judge the one present-ly accused—a traitor. You must decide and pronounce judgement."

Harfan was right. How could Cary accept the intru-sion of a rat joined to the rebellion, spouting names and accusations without evidence? The evidence confirmed the Changeling's guilt as obviously as catching Gregory pilfering his dresser drawers.

Besides, Cary thought, *I'm only judging birds, not hu-mans. This nightmare could be over tomorrow. Then I'll be back on the Fragile Lands, back home, back to normal.*

Cary spoke in a formal tone. "I pronounce the Change-ling guilty of treason to Vangorfold,"

There, I've said it, Cary thought, relieved. *It's over.*

The council conferred briefly and pronounced its sen-tence, to the absolute silence of the court.

"Changeling, you have been found guilty of treason. You will be rendered flightless and imprisoned."

Immediately, two of the council gulls approached the accused bird. With the help of two guards, each gull snapped its beak on the Changeling's outstretched wing and tugged two large primary feathers from the tip, then the four outermost tail feathers. Cary winced.

The pulled feathers lay strewn on the stone floor. Cary sat bolt upright, Unlike the other birds who had been tried that day, he had not asked the Changeling any ques-tions, but it was too late. He slouched back against the seat. The sentence was passed.

Cary quickly reviewed the overwhelming evidence that had been brought forward. It was his duty, as judge, only to decide on the evidence if this bird was a leader of the insurrection or not. It was not his responsibility to decide the punishment. He had not written the Birdfolc laws.

Unlike the previous cases, the assembly of birds remained silent as the Changeling was escorted from the court to his imprisonment.

Cary was exhausted. The last case had sapped his remaining strength. Harfan dismissed the crowd of silent witnesses with an oath. Folclaguhaus, the day of court, was finished.

After the Birdfolc were dismissed and the root tower emptied of all but a few attendants and the council, Cary was invited to sit in a wicker seat. He was carried by tethers to an upper bower, a chamber with a platform floor embedded in the thick root wall of the tower. This held a door at its entry way from the inside, as well as a large portal to the outside world. The leader's bowers, such as this one, also held a crude wooden table, along with an elaborate round bed much like a nest.

Cary ate absentmindedly, his weary mind fixed on the memories of the day. Then he lay down in his nest-bed and instantly fell asleep.

The next morning as he awoke, his bower was brighter with the morning light. Cary's mood, however, did not match the newness of the day. The events of the previous day had tried and tired him. The trial of the Changeling, or this so-called "Adarel," clung to his mind.

He picked at the morning meal that had been delivered to his table. Cary was not so sure he wanted to be a ruler if it meant more of what he had endured the day before. Sitting on a throne, observing ceremonies, accepting gifts and tribute and pronouncing wise judgements were the well-rehearsed imaginings of Cary's royal ambitions, images that did not match the events etched into his memory.

After eating, he walked from the crude wooden table to the glassless window. There were no signs of a nearby town, roadway or even a path. The grey tower of strange giant roots was out of time and place.

Between the long trunks that braced the canopy, Cary surveyed the countryside ablaze in the morning sunlight. His eyes wandered over grass-covered hills and leapt to the darkened edge of a forest looming behind, oddly similar to the view from his grandmother's house on the Fragile Lands, a house full of Cary's best memories.

If it weren't for the pickpocket having to be there too, Cary thought, *Mr. Everybody's Favourite.*

A tapping sound interrupted his thoughts. Cary turned to find a bird, half his height, trying to get his attention by tapping its beak on the table. It lifted up the tray with flat, paddle-like feathers concealed among its primary feathers of each wing. Cary recalled how the council gulls each had long swords in the same place. *Do all the birds have those?*

"I trust you slept well, under the circumstances?" Unannounced, Harfan had passed the threshold of Cary's bower.

"I did sleep," answered Cary. The servant left with the tray.

"And your morning meal? Was it ... satisfactory?"

"Yes ... thank you."

Harfan continued, "You have taken your first flight as Ascentor of Vangorfold. Not withstanding a few ... bumps along the way, you have fulfilled your ... responsibilities to Folclaguhaus well. Our next day of justice will not be for many turns of the earth. This day forward your duties shall be..." Harfan broke off to collect his thoughts. "Yes., To familiarize yourself with Vangorfold ... its folc, its territories and its ... troubles."

"Troubles?" asked Cary.

"The traitor you judged yesterday was the leader of a rebellion. Many times and turns of the earth have passed since Stinga the Backstabber, or Mandwar as a few name him, the head of the insurrection, rebelled against our protector, Wisefaest, in an ambitious attempt to seize the throne. Stinga's wild accusations and lies only led to his exile, where he has since been joined by wanderers, malcontents and thieves. The insurrection has now grown large enough to pose a threat to Vangorfold. Our attention ... and duties lay primarily in crushing the rebellion. I have provided a few scrolls and maps of our territories along with records of past skirmishes. Scrim will assist you."

The same small, dark bird that had testified against the Changeling stepped from behind Harfan, as if it had been cloaked under Harfan's wing, a quiver of rolled bark full of scrolls slung from its beak.

"Should you need help."

Scrim said nothing but turned a beady eye on different points around Cary's bower.

"I'm not hiding anything," said Cary.

Cary slipped the scrolls from Scrim's beak and placed them on the crude wooden table. He had some interest in maps, so he was eager to unroll the parchments.

Harfan was about to take his leave.

"Am I going to be able to see the territories?" asked Cary, "I mean—fly over them?"

"In time," answered Harfan. "At present you must carry out your duties from here. Later, you will meet council."

"Have you found out anything about my sister and brother?" asked Cary. Harfan had jumped onto the sill of the porthole window with a single beat of his wing.

"You will be the first to receive word when we do," assured Harfan.

Harfan dipped his beak to Scrim, draped his wings and with a couple of strong flaps, launched through the opening to the outside world. Cary moved toward the portal. Where was Harfan going? Harfan shrank to a dot on the horizon, where he was joined by another.

Remembering that Scrim had remained behind, Cary politely dismissed the ill-tempered bird. After cocking an eye to several crooks and hollows around the bower, Scrim obeyed and left by the thick wooden door.

Cary sat down and unravelled one of the scrolls. The first scroll was a map, which he quickly surveyed for anything familiar. Several more maps followed.

On one of the maps Cary identified his location. He was at Vangorfold, a stronghold located at the south end of an island. The Muna Mountains, which stretched along the west side of the entire island, was the same range of mountains he had seen when his captors delivered him the day before. Surrounding the island was the Mirror Sea. Nothing on the maps indicated anything beyond. To the Northeast, beyond the Watcher's Wood, were the high cliffs of Husgard Hellir, the stronghold where Mandwar and his followers had taken refuge.

Cary's concentrated study of the maps made his lunch, unlike the grumbling Scrim who had carried it, a welcome sight. Scrim stuck his beak into every gap and hollow formed by the knotted roots and returned to his post outside the door. Cary ate and drank, tracing the maps with his finger wherever his interest led him. After his late lunch, he cradled his head in his arms and fell asleep over his colourful images of mountains, rivers, fields and fen.

CHAPTER EIGHT
Second Thoughts

When Cary awoke, the setting sun was casting a dull orange glow on the criss-cross of large trunk-sized roots on the far side of his bower, including part of the wooden door, which led to the core of the tower stronghold. Cary had planned to walk around and talk with some of the Birdfolc. He walked across his bower and slowly pulled open the door. A shadow cut off the swath of orange light a foot beyond the door. Cary took a few cautious steps. A wing flashed in front of him, pressing him back on his heels.

"You may not pass here!"

It was Scrim.

"I just want to look around."

"Step back!" ordered Scrim.

Cary obeyed. He sucked in a breath and swallowed. Beyond Scrim there were no stairs, no ladders or even a winding root that could lead him below. Two more steps and he would have plummeted straight to the stone bottom.

"There is no passage down," rasped Scrim. "You must

return to your bower."

Cary retreated, thankful the stern-faced Scrim did not follow but had stayed outside where Harfan had posted him. Cary sat down at the table strewn with maps.

Of course, birds would not need stairs, Cary thought.

He concluded it had just been a oversight putting him up so high. Harfan had been simply treating him like any other bird. But another possibility entered Cary's mind: Harfan could have placed him at this height to isolate him, because the old grey bird did not want Cary snooping around.

"But I'm an Ascentor now," whispered Cary to himself. "I can give orders. I'll ask for a lower bower tomorrow."

Comforted by his plan, he retreated to his nest-bed and wondered what he would have to do at his first day at the Watch, the Vangorfold council. He imagined the thrill of being flown over Vangorfold and saluted by underlings.

For the next few days, birds lowered Cary from his bower to meet his council and listen to news about the island. But he never got the chance to contribute anything. In his bower he read more scrolls and studied more maps, but not one bird offered to take him on a flight around the stronghold. Frustrated, Cary requested a lower bower, but council refused, arguing he would be better protected higher off the ground. He was beginning to feel as trapped and bored as his worst days imprisoned in a classroom at school.

Days later, following his evening routine of studying maps and reading Birdfolc history till the last of the candle wicks extinguished in a molten puddle of beeswax, Cary went to sleep.

He fell into a dream. He was on a beach. A dull-witted

seagull knocked him over, mercilessly clamped its long beak onto his big toe and, in lurch after lurch, dragged him along the beach. The gull ignored Cary's frantic orders to let him go. Cary twisted and shouted, desperately trying to pull away his foot. Sweat was dripping into his eyes. He squinted through his stinging eyes to the end of the beach. In unison, a huddle of gulls turned their greedy eyes in his direction, tongues lolling from the sides of their beaks like dogs'.

"They're going to tear me to pieces."

Cary cried out and woke up. As still as a ghastly scarecrow, Scrim was standing at the foot of his bed.

Cary collected himself and assured Scrim he had only had a nightmare. The bird slowly retreated to his post, eyeing the dark cavities created by the intersecting roots that formed the vaulted ceiling of Cary's bower. Cary flopped back on his bed and wiped the sweat from his forehead. He replayed the nightmare over and over and finally shook his head as if to flush out the fiercely beaked gulls.

He sat up to be sure Scrim was not lurking by the doorway. Satisfied that Scrim had likely flown to the opposite side of the tower, perhaps to talk to another bird, Cary's eyes wandered into the darkest hollows of the bower. In one recess two pale yellow spots floated in the dark like tiny moons. The moment Cary leaned forward, the two yellow lights vanished.

Having often teased Gregory for being afraid of the dark, he didn't call Scrim. Nor did he get out of his bed. Instead, he propped up his back and patrolled the dark for any movement or flickers of the hovering yellow moons until his chin nodded against his chest.

In the twilight of sleep, unconscious of how much time had passed, a whisper breezed into his ear.

"Do not make a sound. I come with news of Clarisse and Gregory."

Neither asleep nor fully awake, Cary sat up. At the edge of his nest bed, half in shadow, was a long-snouted rat, the same grinning rat that had interrupted the proceedings at Folclaguhaus. Cary scrambled to his knees.

"I bring these as token," said the rat before Cary could find anything to defend himself.

The rat held out each of his long palms. In his left was the small pouch embroidered with the golden feather.

Gregory must have stashed it in his pocket just before the whirlwind, thought Cary.

In the other was a ring. It was Clarisse's ring, an antique, with a small sapphire. She never removed it from her finger, because it had been a gift from their grandmother. This rat had met Gregory and Clarisse and Clarisse had trusted him, or—Cary did not want to think the worst—the rat had forced it from her.

"What have you done with my sister?" whispered Cary fiercely.

"Done? I have done nothing. Your brother and sister are in the care of Mandwar," answered the rat, rotating its large ear toward the bower door, Scrim possibly on the other side.

"Don't you mean Stinga?" countered Cary.

"No, Earth-dweller, I mean Mandwar, Guardian of Husgard Hellir. You can leave that lie here, in the dark, where it belongs."

Rats in general and some rats in particular, like this rat, could be very argumentative, even in times of great peril.

"You have received the tokens. Now you must come with me," hissed the rat. "Clarisse cautioned me you would be stubborn."

"Stubborn?" said Cary, almost breaking his whisper. "Why should I come with you? Bring my sister and brother here."

"Did you hear anything I said at Adarel's trial? Old Scarecrow—Harfan—is your enemy. Why do you think he has you kept in this tower? For the view?" The rat challenged Cary, his long snout uncomfortably close, his long yellow teeth catching the moonlight.

Cary was silent. He had considered the same possibility. Was Scrim a sour-mouthed bodyguard or a prison guard? And why had Harfan so easily consented to an unknown Earth-dweller taking over? Wasn't the old crow the leader? Cary remembered his reception at the stronghold and the scowling faces of the gulls.

"You must choose," said the rat. "Answers will follow."

Cary slowly climbed out of his nest-bed. The rat moved silently around to meet him. The rat padded to the bed and arranged the quilted cover into a long, crooked lump, took some dark leaves from his satchel and arranged them at the head.

"Follow me."

On the soft pads of his two back feet, his long nails retracted, his long tail trailing like a question mark, the rat cat-stepped to a dark, triangular recess between intersecting roots.

"Are we just going to hide here?" whispered Cary, immediately thinking his question was a stupid one.

"Do you think only birds travel the island? I have been

here as long as the birds and sped over more trails below the wing of a bird than a fox. A rat treads where a bird trembles." The rat whispered quickly, "There will be no light. Hold on to my tail—it will be the last and only time you will do so. When you feel it move to the right, you step right, left—left, down—down. Do you understand?"

"Yes," answered Cary, the black hole gaping before him like a bottomless pit.

They waded into the dark. Cary moved his hand toward his face. His finger was swallowed in black, even as it touched his nose. The rat had led Cary into the labyrinth of roots that formed the tower's shell, a natural wall so impenetrably thick and tangled that most of its bowers had to be constructed on the inside, like round shelves of fungus perched over the stronghold's keep.

The rat's tail gripped in his right hand, Cary sent his left hand, like a tentative insect's feeler, in search of any guiding surface. "If you pull my tail any harder, you will pluck it like a feather," hissed the rat, a little louder than he had before. "Give it some slack! One misstep, and you will have us both in a pinch."

"What's your name?" queried Cary. "Unless you want me to call you Mr. Rat."

"Fyrndagas Underdel Dearth ... the Third," hissed the rat. "Mark what happens if you call me Missster Rat again."

Cary felt the rat's breath on his cheek.

"If you cannot manage to remember the title, Earth-dweller, try Dearth."

CHAPTER NINE
Gregory's Gift

In the next few days, as Birdfolc described the passage of days at Husgard, Gregory came to like Ofost as if she were another sister. Likewise, Ofost had felt responsible for Gregory ever since she safely delivered him to Husgard and so became his constant companion.

"How do you keep the sword from slipping out?" asked Gregory.

"It has replaced one of my feathers," replied Ofost. "Look here." Ofost spread her wing and revealed the place where the sword was attached. Gregory drew close to her open, splayed feathers.

"The colours on your feathers ... they're shimmering. Do you have a hand?" asked Gregory.

"No, but we can move a feather or two on each wing, like a wrist. All Birdfolc have special wings, which can be fitted, or pinioned," said Ofost. "Some have been fitted with tools; others have swords, like me."

"But our birds don't," said Gregory.

"No, just Birdfolc," said Ofost.

"How do you use the sword? Show me."

Ofost backed away from Gregory and poked her head through the passageway door to be sure no attendant stood near. She returned and extended both her wings to her sides, dropping two or three lower feathers on either side to form a shield or wing-guard. A long, golden sword shaped like a primary feather, only more slender, extended straight out from each wing. It glinted in the soft golden light.

Standing well back from Gregory, Ofost swept one sword down in front of her. After she flashed a dramatic, fierce eye at Gregory, down swept the other. Her slender swords cut the air in a flurry of whispers and whistles.

"Again, again!" urged Gregory.

"Very good form," said Mandwar as he drew up behind Ofost. "But I do not need my feathers trimmed this evening."

Ofost, as startled as Gregory when he was caught borrowing, gave a little bow as she moved to the side to let Mandwar pass.

"Aevi and I have some business to attend to this evening," said Mandwar. "Gren has been asking for you, Ofost. I believe he is posted in the passageway near Clarisse's chamber at this time."

Ofost left to find Gren.

"Now, little Aevi, come with me."

Gregory walked with the old owl down a corridor, chatting up the owl like an owlet with too many questions. As the odd pair followed the passageways that led deeper into Husgard, the golden threads on the walls and ceiling multiplied, converging in a single chamber. Gregory and Mandwar entered. The golden branches in the chamber spread upward to form a densely woven dome. *I couldn't even squeeze through*, Gregory thought. He felt as if he were under the canopy of a great old tree, like the old oak where he had found the pouch in the park.

"Walk under the dome, little one," instructed the owl. "Look up and tell me what you see."

Gregory walked to the centre of the stone floor spread with trailing golden roots like the great canopy of branches overhead. He stood in front of a flat-topped pedestal, like a trunk that had been sawn off, embossed with feathers. He wanted to reach up to the canopy and touch the shimmering branches, but the golden braids were twice the owl's height and out of reach. The owl motioned with his large, glittering eyes toward the roof of branches.

Mandwar waited while Gregory explored the canopy. His curiosity satisfied, Gregory stopped and concentrated his gaze near the canopy's highest point.

"What do you see?" asked Mandwar.

Gregory, who had not been following the branches but examining the dark spaces between, said, "I think I see stars in a night sky."

"Excellent," Mandwar said. "Keep looking."

Something caught Gregory's eye.

"Now, what do you see?" asked Mandwar.

"It looks like clouds—no—shadows of things moving behind the branches."

"Things?"

"Like people running around," continued Gregory, "looking for something."

Gregory startled. "I see a—a rat! It's running through a dark tunnel. Someone is following it—pulling its tail. I think someone is trying to catch the rat."

"Good. Excellent. And this your first peek into times passing."

Mandwar chirped an excited exclamation in the old tongue. Gregory broke his gaze. The spaces between the beautiful golden branches transformed to stone.

"Come, Aevi," beckoned Mandwar, extending a large wing. "You have seen a marvellous thing. Your brother is on the run from Harfan, the old Scarecrow of Vangorfold, but not to worry. He is with Fyrndagas Dearth, a most exceptional rat if ever there was one. He will lead your brother here."

"Can I tell Clarisse?" asked Gregory.

"When the moon has fled, little one, tomorrow. Let your sister rest. She has been very busy."

As mentor and novice exited the large chamber of golden branches, Ofost ducked into the passageway, Gren following. They were in close conversation.

"Later, you shall see the Dome of Times Passing again," said Mandwar. "Now, you must rest. Ofost will escort you to your chamber."

"Ofost, come and escort young Aevi to his chamber and see that he is comfortable, and if this marvellous, eagle-eyed boy should be hungry, be sure that he is well fed," said the greying owl as he turned to walk down a passageway.

"Where is he going?" asked Gregory.

"I have not often seen him walk so fast. He will do that now and again." Ofost lowered her voice. "Husgard business! is what he usually says and totters off."

Gregory watched Mandwar leave, not quite as happy as when he first came into the passageway beside the kindly owl.

"Not to worry," said Ofost. "Mandwar will be back. Maybe you will see him again tomorrow. How do you like your nest?"

"My nest?" asked Gregory. "In Clarisse's room?"

"I am sorry, Aevi. I fear your nest has been moved. It is above the ground, like a nest in a tree. You will find it in your own chamber, but I am not sure if you can sleep in it tonight."

"Why?" asked Gregory.

"I do not think you have the skill to climb the rope ladder," Ofost replied.

"Yes, I can. Watch me. Take me to the nest—please. I'll show you."

"This way, master Aevi. We shall see," said Ofost, as she led her enthusiastic charge down the passageway.

When Gregory arrived at the chamber arranged for him, he proved quickly quite able to climb into his nest.

"See! See! I'm a bird," exulted Gregory, his arms stretched wide for soaring.

"No doubt you will soon be sprouting wings," said Ofost.

Gregory lay back in his comfortable nest. He was much closer to the veins of gold running along the stone ceiling of his chamber, just a few arm lengths away. When he began following its intricate patterns, Ofost suggested a song. In answer, Gregory pulled himself up to the edge of his nest-bed.

Ofost fluted a playful tune that reminded him of the birds flitting through the trees in the spring outside his window. Like a deepening stream, the melody's currents slowed and deepened in pitch. Gregory leaned back in his bed, his face to the ceiling. The song mingled with the elaborate maze of gold that wove through the quartz. It cheered Gregory with all the power of the forest and its living creatures. He drifted into sleep, imagining himself in a hazy meadow on a wonderful picnic.

Ofost quietly left the slumbering Gregory to join Gren, since both guessed Mandwar would summon leaders to discuss new developments.

It did not often happen that Mandwar was so pleased. There could be no doubt about the images Gregory had seen and described. Fyrndagas Underdel Dearth was leading Cary through Vangorfold's underground.

Mandwar told Ofost and Gren to fly to the rendezvous point Dearth had arranged. The two warriors were also to report any word by fur or feather of Vaskar, who had not been seen since his capture.

Ofost and Gren left Mandwar and flew to a stoop at the very top of the cliff that sheltered Husgard. The experienced scouts searched the wooded landscape far below and the sky above.

At night, the golden branches throughout the passageways of Husgard dimmed. The bright, golden-fringed feathers of Ofost and Gren softened in the same way. In fact, the underside of the Gildenhyrn's wings shimmered like ripples in an evening pool against the dark navy blue sky. The perfect camouflage.

In a few moments, without a word or an audible flap of a wing, the two Gildenhyrn warriors launched from the cliff on Mandwar's appointed task.

CHAPTER TEN

Into the Dark

In the dark, Cary straddled, crawled under and squeezed between an endless tangle of unseen roots and tubers. After the hard lessons of a few head-knocks, bruised shins and abrupt orders from Dearth, such as "Stop pulling my tail!" or "Keep your left hand in front," Cary grew accustomed to the gentle pressure of the rat's tail pushing against his cold hand, and Dearth got better at timing his directions, so Cary less often bumped his head, knocked a shoulder or banged a shin.

When Cary wondered if he would ever escape the never-ending nightmare of tangled roots, his thankful feet met solid flat rock. Dripping water echoed against stone walls. Cary had followed Dearth into a large underground cavern. Ascentor and spy had, in fact, come into a network of dungeons beneath Vangorfold, lost to this time passing. Here, Fyrndagas Dearth decided to rest.

"Birds never come here," whispered Dearth, "too

deep—dark tunnels. The Birdfolc of Vangorfold have others do their dungeon work. Put this on—quickly," urged the rat, handing Cary what felt like a black rubbery coat that went down past his knees. The rat must have stashed the coat before its climb up the tower wall. Cary struggled putting on the coat in the dark. It was a little big, crudely sewn together and smelled like fresh leaves.

"You will need it here," whispered the rat. " Dearth took hold of Cary's arm. "Sit down here. Hold out your hand. Eat this."

The damp vault smelled of mould and wet. The darkness was total. Cary dared not rest his back against the unseen cavern wall. The crawling things that hid here were better left undisturbed.

He was happy to sit in the dark and rest, thinking of nothing but the dull crunch of a few stale nuts and a root that tasted of bitter carrot. His neck was sore. He had held his head low for fear of cracking it against a low, overhanging root, which Dearth always avoided. Cary leaned forward, put his elbows on his knees and cradled his head.

When he shifted his weight, his right foot dislodged something beside his foot. Curious, but not enough to use his hand, Cary lifted his foot and gently nudged the thing aside. A pale clank interrupted the silent dark. Cautiously, Cary reached down in exactly the direction of the sound so he would not touch anything else. His fingers alighted on what felt like rock, but as he explored further, he traced a large round link of scabbed metal, which made a loop big enough to pass through his hand. He gently tried to lift it, but it resisted. "Must be joined with other links." Cary decided he had better set it down before he got into trouble with his sharp-tongued escort, so he lowered the large link of cold, rough metal to the stone floor. When the large link reached the floor, it lodged on its side, locked by links on either side.

"What are you at?" whispered Dearth.

"Nothing," answered Cary. "I knocked my foot against something."

"We do not have far to go. The passage is straight from here. Take hold of my tail. We have to go. Watch your head."

When Cary stood up, he could already feel the stiffness in his back from having walked in a crouched position for so long. He reached ahead in the darkness, feeling for Dearth's tail. With the tail gently in his grip, he warily reached out his left hand to find the slimy stone with the tips of his fingers.

At the exact moment the oozing passageway wall met his fingertips, a deep clank rang from the stone floor.

"What was that?" whispered Dearth. "What were you playing at?"

"Something metal," Cary answered. "Part of a chain, I think."

"Shhh!" Dearth and Cary stood like stone, listening to the hushed darkness.

Far down another passageway, something ground and grated as if it had been dragged over the stone floor. Before Cary's next breath, a few more metallic clanks echoed into the darkness, as if chain links had settled onto one another farther away.

"Come! I do not want to meet whatever is at the end of that chain." Dearth swept his tail into Cary's face.

Cary's heart began to pound in his ears like a drum.

I'm behind the rat, Cary thought, one hand too tightly

gripped on Dearth's tail. *Whatever is at the end of that chain, if it catches us, it'll sink its teeth into me first.*

Drips and the sound of footfalls filled the dark. During Cary's next slow exhale, the chain, as if thrown aside, crashed against rock. He jerked around toward the metallic clamour. Dearth had also stopped to judge its distance. But not for long. Cary's guide strode forward again at a quicker pace. The long fingers of the foul darkness pawed at Cary's back. Three times he threw his chin over his shoulder to scour the stalking dark, stuttering his steps.

"Your dancing is slowing us down! Eyes forward," Dearth hissed.

But Cary could not help himself. Terror had gripped him. He strained his eyes in the darkness. Far down the passageway a dull orange light illuminated the tunnel walls.

"Something's coming!" Cary whispered.

"Of course," said Dearth. "With those heavy footfalls of yours, we must have alarmed every living beast that ever crawled underground."

The terrible news provided a hint of what Cary needed most: light. The dim glow from the straight passageway provided enough light to highlight the edges of stoops, overhangs and threatening outcrops of rock. Cary was able to move faster, to the great relief of his frustrated rescuer.

Although he would never have shown it or admitted it, the brave Fyrndagas Underdel Dearth the Third bore a fear. Dearth did not fear many enemies. Dogs were clumsy, and cats, though sly and fast, were generally lazy, two nuisances easily evaded. Owls and other predators of the sky could be avoided with experience, but snakes—

snakes made Dearth's kind shudder. Snakes were subtle, deathly quiet and quietly deadly, and Fyrndagas Underdel Dearth, his rat nose twitching in the dark, had unmistakably smelled a snake. Its reek had stung his keenly sensitive nostrils, but Dearth was puzzled. How could I have missed that stench in times past?

Neither could envision the terror that had awakened, once entombed in stone, lying unseen, motionless, under an enchantment for many times passing. But it was not Cary who had disturbed the creature, but its keeper.

Cary and Dearth passed into a tall cavern, dully lit by cracks in the stone high above like a cathedral. Cary followed Dearth down a natural wide stairway of unevenly spaced steps. Above them, filling the entranceway in the cavern wall, the brightening orange glow glistened off the wet stone. In a few moments the head of the creature dragging the chain would emerge from the tunnel. Dearth reached the end of the stair first and leapt across the wide floor.

"Through here," ordered Dearth.

Dearth had already squeezed through vertical bars a few feet into a tunnel. How had he done it? Cary passed an arm through, then his shoulder, but his head was too big. In a panic, he retrieved his limbs.

Cary crouched down and shuffled along the chamber's irregularly carved wall, sweeping his hand over the stones, searching for any crevice, any crack to hide in— nothing. Another six feet and his hand slipped into an empty space, not high, maybe a foot rising from the floor, an arm's length wide. Cary tore off his coat and lay down on his stomach. He pushed himself back feet first into the hole until his legs flopped down. With outstretched feet, he probed for the bottom. The arched entrance leading to the sloping stairway was glowing like a lit fireplace. Whatever it was, the thing would crawl or slither out in seconds. He pushed himself further in. His feet touched the bottom. He snatched his coat and dropped down into the hole.

Cary swung his arm to gauge the size of the hole. Beside him and behind, his arm swung into empty space. He spidered his fingers along the floor toward the back. He found an edge at an arm's length, felt around for a loose stone and tossed it into the darkness. Not a sound. Seconds later, distant cracks echoed from the depths below as the stone bounced from rock to rock. He was on a shelf, a narrow ledge inches from a long drop into a cavernous pit.

If it has a head small enough to squeeze through the hole, thought Cary, *I'm dead.*

In his terror, he had an idea. He eased down onto his knees, covered himself with his coat and hugged the rock wall.

Maybe I'll look like a rock.

Cary waited, his breathing ferociously loud and heavy under the rubbery coat. He was suffocating; he had to breathe. He gently lifted the edge of the coat, exposing his face to fresher air. The edges of the hole above him were fringed in an orange glow. The light was moving around the edges of the hole, as if a car were slowly driving by. Whatever it was, it had entered the lower chamber.

The glow became brighter. Cary flipped the coat back over his head and counted, fifteen, sixteen. When he reached twenty, he would ease his eyes over the edge— Eighteen, nineteen, twenty. He slid the coat back. The orange glow had faded.

His coat over his head as in a rainstorm, he slid his chin up the rock, edging the tip of his nose closer to the bottom lip of the opening. Slowly, the cavernous underground chamber came into view. He followed the uppermost section of the far wall of the cavern down to the darkened archway and sloping stairway.

As if being kidnapped from his home by armoured birds was not frightening enough, now the terrors of his storybooks were springing to life. Dragging its chain up the steps link by link, a wide collar of iron tight behind its jaws, its scaly black body ringed with glowing orange bands, its long black bat-like wings tight along its side, slid a giant, glistening serpent.

When its head reached the top, it turned its wide, slick head toward the cavern below. Its long forked tongue flickered out, tasting the air. Its yellow black-slitted eye darted in precise jerks, surveying the cavern floor. Cary ducked down. When he found the courage to raise his head again, the last glowing rings of the snake's tail wormed through the archway, its grating chain obediently following.

With the little light that remained, Cary scrambled out of the hole back to the barred tunnel that had almost trapped him. He risked a short call into the gloom.

"Dearth!"

Judging by his own ability to contort and compress himself into a hole of almost any size, Dearth had made an understandable miscalculation in the width of the bars. He had returned to the bars too late to help. Cary was gone. Had Cary been trapped, Dearth would have challenged any beast without hesitation, even a giant snake. Hoping that Cary had found even the tiniest of hiding places, Dearth had stayed by the grate, making noises to distract the serpent, convincing the glowing snake that its quarry had escaped through the bars and into the tunnel. Dearth had wagered his pelt the winged serpent could not breathe fire.

Cary could not pass through the grate on his second attempt any more easily than the first. Dearth had to do the unthinkable. He exited the barred tunnel and ascended the wide, sloping stairway, his whiskers twitching at the serpent's foul odour. After motioning to Cary to follow, Dearth, on all fours, crept through the darkened archway.

Scouting ahead, Dearth led Cary slowly down the passage to another smaller tunnel. It would prove a tight fit for an overgrown snake.

"I saw it," Cary whispered, unable to contain his discovery.

"Keep it to yourself," answered Dearth. "Any more noise from you, and we'll both end up down a snake's gullet!"

"You know it's a snake?" asked Cary, surprised.

"No mistaking the stench. Now keep quiet!"

Cary could not smell anything but the damp. He followed Dearth, tail in hand, as before. After many tentative toe-to-heel steps through the dark, a wave of cold fresh sea air swirled past Cary. He was relieved, but Dearth was worried. Ahead was another set of bars, although, if Dearth's memory served him correctly, the stone in which the bars were anchored had begun to crumble.

The weary and wary travellers continued on light feet, Cary checking behind for any hint of an orange glow and Dearth prodding Cary to keep his nose pointed in the right direction. Finally, they entered a small cell, partially lit in a streak of blue white light, old straw scattered across the floor.

"Some poor creature has inhabited this cell a short time ago," said Dearth. "These are the outer cells. We must be vigilant."

"Who built this," asked Cary. "I mean, the dungeons and the tower."

"Built? No one. Birds have built nests and other creatures their dens, but the tower grew of itself. It was once a great tree. The largest on the island.

Dearth moved to the source of moonlight, a small rectangular opening at the top of the wall, but just above the level of the ground outside. After a careful check for patrol guards, Dearth inspected the bars. One of the bars could be turned. With hurried scratches from Dearth and a few two-handed tugs from Cary, the upper end of the bar moved far enough back to pull the bar from the sill.

"Now we must wait. The guards will report at sunrise."

"What about the tower?" asked Cary.

"In a time past, seeds were dropped in the great tree's canopy. They grew, unseen. When the seedlings leafed and dropped their roots, every creature believed its new vines had been produced by the great tree. That was in a time past, an age of conflict among Birdfolc, a conflict that began in the Fragile Lands."

Dearth trailed off after a memory.

"It is a long tale or a short one, but the short of it is there was sorcery in it. The seeds had been sown by an enemy. Its roots strangled the tree; the tree perished. The root shell stands. So is the shorter history of Vangorfold Stronghold."

Dearth checked at the grate. "We must move quickly."

Dearth went through first. Cary followed.

"We are out," whispered Dearth, sniffing the cool morning air, "but not out of danger."

CHAPTER ELEVEN

An Unexpected Rescue

Ofost and Gren flew higher than any bird dared, wingtip to wingtip, surveying the skies above the Watcher's Wood and the eastern reaches of the golden fields.

"We should form a rescue squad, attack Vangorfold and free Adarel," said Gren.

"But he forbade an attack."

"Yes, he forbade it, but we are free to choose," Gren responded.

"Free to choose what's right," said Ofost, easily catching up Gren, who had darted ahead, ruffled by Ofost's last remark. "Adarel wants to unite all folc under the Song of Fridorfold. Many folc in Vangorfold are obedient to Harfan, out of fear or deceit. You do remember what Adarel has taught us."

"Yes, yes, Win birds before battles, but what did he gain in exchange for his imprisonment? The freedom of over two hundred birds on whose loyalty we cannot depend."

"Those Birdfolc were held in Vangorfold territory under threat of old Scarecrow. The folc had families, Gren.

The Vultori caught them trying to cross into Husgard territory. So Adarel made the pact. His..."

"His captivity for his folcs' freedom," interrupted Gren. "The Song and the singing will be lost."

"It may be," said Ofost, "like the Nightingale, the singer sings best from his cage. Can you compare the singing of Adarel to the threats of Harfan? The captives he freed will not forget; he has brought the Song of Fridorfold to the folc of Vangorfold. Adarel knows what he is doing."

"Who will save Husgard?" Gren objected. "We are the last hope of Fridorfold. Mandwar is doing all he can, but we are outnumbered on land and in the sky."

"We have the three, the Ascentors," said Ofost.

"The Ascentors are young," he said. "How will..."

"When Adarel appointed you to the Gildenhyrn, how old were you?" asked Ofost.

Gren flew on in silence. Ofost's remark had hit its mark.

"The Song will go on," said Ofost. "He is Adarel, a Singer of Ellri from times past and times passing when the Song of Fridorfold was first sung."

"You are beginning to sound like my teacher, Ofost," Gren chided.

"In speed, I shall always be your teacher," said Ofost as she fell into a dead drop.

Accepting her challenge, Gren rolled into a dive. The two Gildenhyrn reached a speed where a misplaced wingtip could send a bird into a spill. When the two golden arrows neared the brink of tumbling into a fluttering mass of flopping wings and feathers, the expert flyers abruptly pulled up. No bird could have matched the pair's speed or have seen the descent.

"This is our rendezvous point." Ofost and Gren flew

for the highest branches in the broad canopy of an old tree. The scouts were on the border of the northern edge of the Fridorian Pass, the Vangorian Pass under Harfan's rule, old Scarecrow's territory. Gren and Ofost watched and waited in silence.

In less than an hour, voices approached from the ground a short distance away.

"You volunteered for the task. It will put us in line for a promotion, promotion, you said. Now, Chirrup, you want to pull out, out. You're an earth-bound chicken," one voice said.

"Well, let's to it, let's to it. Get it over with. He's as good, as good as dead anyway," said the other voice.

Not far from the tree where Ofost and Gren had alighted, two starlings approached, walking on either side of an old raccoon trundling a cart. In the cart under a tarp was a bulge.

"Stop the cart. Here is as good a place as ever, as ever," said the first starling. "Pull him off."

The other starling approached the back of the cart, grabbed the tarpaulin with its beak and started tugging at it.

"Wait," ordered the first voice. "Look around, Chirrup, and make sure the area is clear of mischief."

The other bird complied, flying low through the surrounding trees. The bird returned in a wingbeat.

"Clear, clear," the starling said. The starlings removed the rough tarp.

"It's Vaskar!" Gren said, forgetting himself.

One of the two starlings on the ground stopped and cocked his head. In quick precise jerks, he tilted an eye to high branches and low bushes, its pinioned swords at the ready. "Did you hear something? Did you hear?"

"No, let's get on with it, Chirrup," said the second.

The two starlings did not have the chance to argue with each other again. Ofost and Gren, golden swords brandished, swooped down.

The first starling foolishly met Gren's challenge. In a whisper from the Gildenhyrn's sword, the starling lost his black sword and the tips of his flight feathers. The other starling fled at full speed through the trees, with Ofost giving chase. The pursuit did not last long before Ofost had the bird pinned under her talons, the terrified bird squawking like a chicken about to be plucked.

"Send this to Harfan with our compliments," said Ofost as she produced a small golden feather as token. With that, she plucked a few tail feathers from the panicked bird, and with one more squawk, let it fly for its life. Because of its missing feathers, the retreating starling flew as if it had been caught in a whirlwind.

"Now what?" asked Ofost as she returned to Gren, who had also let his enemy flee, bearing a token to Harfan.

"He is dying. If I know his captors, they haven't fed Vaskar since he arrived back on Shelter Island carrying Ascentor Arithi's brother, Cary. We must transport him to Mandwar," said Gren, carefully attending to Vaskar's wounds.

"One of us must stay to meet Dearth," said Ofost. "The other must return to Husgard with Vaskar."

"Not with that old raccoon," said Gren. "He won't make the journey in time."

Ofost flew off for help, leaving Gren on guard. Within minutes Ofost returned. "Help is coming." A few investigated noises later, two foxes bounded through the trees, each snatching up a tether attached to the wagon.

"I will accompany Vaskar back to Husgard," offered Ofost.

"And I will wait for Dearth," said Gren. "On the Wings of the Ellri!"

In a moment Ofost had vanished through the trees, scouting ahead of the tireless foxes. Gren returned to his watch high in the tree, ears sharp, eyes surveying, his swords at the ready.

CHAPTER TWELVE

The Wings of Fridorfold

After five days, Clarisse had made many friends among the folc of Husgard, especially the archers. She had been watching over her ever-wandering little brother, who had poked his head into every chamber in the labyrinth of caves.

At the end of the fifth day, after a story or two, once she settled Gregory, Clarisse returned to her chambers and drifted into much-needed sleep.

That night she dreamed she was carrying a large backpack up a mountainside path. As she trudged up the path, her pack began to grow longer with each step. When the pack began to drag on the ground behind her, she decided to remove the burden once and for all. She wrenched her arms back to grab the pack, but felt nothing. She tried to shake it off, but the large, strapless pack only shuffled a bit and returned to its original position.

At the most frustrating point of her dream, at the moment she had begun to panic, Clarisse woke up. She was on her back. She surveyed the ceiling above her nest-bed, following the sparkling, intermingling gold threads. She took a breath of relief, more aware now of her surroundings. It was a dream.

She tried to sit up. But just as if part of her dream had been pulled into the real world, the same strapless packs clung to her back. Unable to sit up, Clarisse rolled onto her left side. The burden pulled at her left shoulder blade, but not the other, so she rolled onto her stomach. Finally, she found some relief from the lumpy load. She pushed herself up onto her hands and knees.

"What's happening to me?" she said. "Am I sick—or paralyzed or something?"

She called out for Gren.

Gren was on a mission with Ofost, but a young attendant came into her chamber the moment she called out. The young bird's round, dark eyes widened, her beak dropped open, and her wings involuntarily popped out to each side. She immediately backed out of the chamber. Clarisse was frightened. Something was wrong.

She stood up and pawed her back. What had clung to her? She grabbed hold of something. It was soft and rigid. Clarisse was desperate. She gripped the clinging burden and pulled with all the strength she had.

"Ow!" Clarisse released her grip.

Mandwar entered her chamber, out of breath.

"Clarisse!"

He startled Clarisse so much, she almost fell over.

"Stand still."

Mandwar approached her, his wings partially unfolded.

"I should have connected the roots to the tree," Mandwar said, almost mumbling. "The golden feathers in the pouch—one of three, and the Song. I should have understood."

"Understood what?" asked an exasperated Clarisse.

"You have sprouted wings, Arithi! Beautiful, glorious, birds-of-a-feather wings!" said Mandwar, extending his wings farther. "And you are taller."

Clarisse had sprouted wings and was now easily the size of Ofost, who would certainly not be able to carry her in her present condition.

She craned her neck, but her body followed. The harder she twisted her head, the more her body turned, until she finally lost her balance and fell into her nest-bed, flat on her back. Mandwar came to her aid, his wings extended. Clarisse took hold of each wing and pulled herself to her feet.

"Grip my wings," said Mandwar. "Now, concentrate on your back. Forget your wings for a moment. Do you feel anything new?"

"Yes, new muscles," answered Clarisse. "Bigger muscles."

"Squeeze your shoulders back," instructed Mandwar. "Good. Now stretch!"

Clarisse complied. She had taken many archery lessons here and at home. Stretching sore back muscles was a necessary routine.

"Good—more — now look to either side," said Mandwar, his voice softening with approval, though no less excited.

Extended to almost twice her height, one tip almost touching the corner of her chamber, draped a beautiful wing, its silken feathers shimmering with the intermingling colours of her red and brown hair.

"I—I have wings," Clarisse said. She sucked in her

breath and shouted, "I have wings!"

I have wings was exactly what Gregory had said, but unlike Clarisse, he neither dreamed about the wings, nor was he frightened. His attendant, who had responded to crashes and excited yelps bursting from Gregory's chamber, darted in. She found Gregory, unsuccessfully, needless to say, trying to fly. Teach me, teach me were his first words to the dumbfounded attendant, who stood as if her claws had rooted in the stone, her eyes blinking at the larger, dishevelled Gregory, the boy's wings going off in different directions as if an extension of his untameable hair.

Some days later, after breathtaking flying lessons under the direction of one of the best flyers of the Gildenhyrn, Clarisse and Gregory were alone together for the first time since arriving at Husgard.

"Did you see me?" asked Gregory, tugging Clarisse's wing. Finding a suitable place to sit down with wings was a new skill. Like a queen with a long train flowing behind her, Clarisse had to accommodate her wings wherever she sat. Gregory paid little heed to his choice of seats and often found himself with wings and legs awkwardly splayed over the floor, adding to his count of purply bruises.

"Do you think Cary has wings, too?" asked Gregory, who had begun to miss his older brother, at least a little.

Clarisse helped Gregory up from the floor for the umpteenth time and sat down next to him on a tapered column that had its point cut off to serve as a perch for Birdfolc.

"I suppose he has. We all had a feather from the pouch."

Clarisse brushed back the hair from Gregory's forehead and straightened an errant feather that had not settled in among the others. "Mandwar said he should have known we would sprout wings. Something about roots to a tree. I heard him talking about misinterpreting some ancient writing or other, which I didn't understand, but after a few mumbles he said it was in the Song."

"Ofost sang me a song," said Gregory. "It made me think of home, and Grandma's."

"The good songs usually do," said Clarisse.

"It made me sleepy," said Gregory, "like sleeping outside on a picnic blanket."

"It's the Song of Fridorfold," said Clarisse.

"Freeterold?"

"No, Free-door-fold," explained Clarisse. "The song's very old and very long. It tells the story of the birds here and their hopes. Now, we are in the song. It says we will help bring back Fridorfold."

"Like the pictures in that other room," added Gregory.

"The Story Weaver's chamber," said Clarisse. "The Song of Fridorfold is like the tapestries in that chamber, but all woven together into one story. I'm only sorry Cary hasn't heard the Song, or at least parts of it." She paused. "I wonder where he is now?"

Where Cary was the moment Clarisse asked her question and where he had been when she and Gregory sprouted wings were two entirely different places. When Clarisse's overwhelming nightmare turned into overpowering, luxurious wings, Cary was somewhere near the middle of Vangorfen, curled up in a small den under the roots of a very large tree.

After travelling most of the night, Dearth had found shelter, the cramped quarters of an abandoned badger hole. The forest had remained unusually quiet for the night, birds or other woodland animals seldom venturing north into the forest for fear of the Vultori, whose desolate home was nearby in the Soltin Crags.

Cary pulled himself from the hole under the tree in what was now the late afternoon the next day. It was much more difficult climbing out than sliding in. His back ached. He supposed his muscles had cramped because he had walked like a crooked cane through Vangorfold Stronghold's tunnels and had slept curled up in a badger's den. His baggy black coat had stretched tight around his chest and was biting into his underarms. When he finally released its snagged buttons, his coat launched above his head and hung over him like a collapsed umbrella.

When Dearth returned with some food he had foraged, he found Cary spinning around as if fire ants had crawled up his back.

"Stop your dancing," Dearth ordered. "Are you trying to attract the attention of every animal in the woods or just every bird over the island?"

"I can't get this stupid coat off."

"That dull-witted coat saved your life," replied Dearth. "Come here."

Cary moved under the protection of the trees.

Dearth hopped on top of a stump. "Stop fidgeting."

Cary did as he was told. Dearth removed the coat.

"You are fortunate you did not grow wings under Vangorfold," said Dearth. "You would have been trapped like a bird in a cage, a snake's dinner. Come over here out of view of the entire countryside and eat."

His rescuer's words filled the air, but did not penetrate Cary's ear. His aching shoulder blades occupied his every thought. He crossed his arms to relieve the throbbing pain.

"Close your wings!" Dearth commanded. Dearth reached up, took hold of the jointed bones so as not to injure the feathers, and deftly folded Cary's wings back behind him. "Come here and sit down."

Cary, numb and dumbfounded, sat on the fallen trunk of a tree. He rolled his shoulders and stretched his back. It was as if two large folding umbrellas, the kind his grandmother put up at the market to sell her honey, had been sewn to his back.

Fyrndagas Underdel Dearth, his long snout as close to Cary's face as possible without touching noses, said, "You have grown wings. You have also grown larger—all the more difficult to keep hidden. Do not—Look at me. Do not try to fly unless you want to betray our position to every Dreygar south of the Golden Fields, who are, no doubt, searching for us as we speak. Sit and collect yourself."

Dearth sat beside Cary and handed him a cut piece of root. Cary sat in silence, frequently tilting back his head. The black wings rooted in his back, folded higher than his head, might well have been dragon wings, or some other hideous appendage attached by a spell.

"I'm turning into a bird," said Cary.

"Unlikely," said Dearth. "Although a beak would be welcome—to muffle the noise."

Cary said nothing but kept stealing glances at his new limbs.

"Take the wings as a gift," said Dearth. "Do not gape at

me. I did not fetter you with your burden. And eat something. We have a long way to go."

Cary trailed behind Dearth as the experienced scout navigated his way through the trees. Unseen behind Dearth, Cary was able to flex his first wing muscles. He tried to unfurl each of his wings out to one side and fold it back.

He felt as if he had another pair of long arms to control. By subtly moving his shoulder blades, he could make his wings respond. The more he moved his new appendages, the more he could sense his wing's position and the controlling muscles. In turn, the new sensations in his back muscles told him what his wings were doing. Though the feathers gave no sensation, their quills felt like the ends of thin pegs penetrating the length of his arm. With concentration and practice he might subtly manipulate a feather's angle, especially the primaries.

In a couple of hours, Cary was able to completely stretch out a wing, retrieve it, and do the same with the other, with complete control.

"I told you to keep your flappers to yourself," Dearth chided when he turned around and caught Cary practicing. Dearth really did not have any appreciation for wings. Cary imagined if the rat had received a pair of his own wings, he would have begged to have them removed.

Dearth understood, however, that the wings were another sign Cary had been chosen as an Ascentor. This made him all the more vigilant in his task of safely delivering Cary to the assigned rendezvous point, where he would release his charge to Ofost and Gren. After that, he would return to what he did best, collecting information from Vangorfold Stronghold and creating as much trouble as possible, confiscating—the term he liked to use—maps, plans, weapons, keys or anything else he could get his paws on.

The revelation of the giant snake in the dungeon presented a problem to Dearth, but not unsolvable. Many tunnels lead to treasure.. No, the trouble did not lie behind, but ahead.

CHAPTER THIRTEEN
Waylaid

Dearth led Cary to a high ridge with a distant view of the rendezvous point to the northeast. From his vantage point, the tops of trees rolled out ahead like a green carpet that ended at its far end in a dark, misty cloud. Dearth said the few birds off in the distance did not present any immediate danger, so the two unlikely companions continued on their long trek through Vangorfen.

The Day of Justice at Vangorfold Stronghold pricked at Cary's conscience. He had been playing out of his league. It was as if he had, without the proper training, without any real experience, stepped into his father's job as anthropologist for a day. The serious nature of the Changeling's trial nettled his conscience the most. Doubts darted in and out of his mind, pestering him like the tiresome flies.

Why hadn't he asked the Changeling direct questions, as he had with the other birds? Why didn't the Changeling defend himself? Why did Harfan try a bird for something as serious as treason together with other minor offences?

Cary's questions succumbed to doubts, leading him on

paths as lonely and winding as the trail through Vangorfen. He recalled Vangorfold, how a thousand birds had raised their voices and named him an Ascentor. He considered the careful plans Dearth and other of Harfan's enemies had to have made to get him out of Vangorfold Stronghold. He had been honoured as an important figure in some great conflict, yet he had never felt so strangely abandoned.

Images of his mom and dad drifted into his mind, carrying him farther down lonely paths. How would recalling his parents, who were usually away or too busy to talk, help now? His dad, especially, might as well be a being from a different planet. Getting to know his dad was like reading about someone in a newspaper. Consciously or not, Cary had concluded that his father was doing a job reserved for the especially talented, definitely not the person who was trudging along behind a rat in the middle of nowhere. He could not even be sure his parents knew he and Clarisse were missing.

His parents had made a significant discovery at an archaeological "dig," charging Cary and Clarisse with babysitting the Pickpocket. A nanny was supposed to drop by for an hour around dinnertime to help oversee operations, as his dad had put it, but she never showed. It was as if the three of them had been kidnapped, and no one noticed, or cared.

As if he were floating lazily down a river only to wake up at the edge of a waterfall, Cary awoke to a dangerous predicament. The leaders at Husgard Hellir, or worse, his sister and brother, would discover that he alone was responsible for the Changeling's punishment.

Cary was thankful to stumble over a root that startled

the crowd of dark thoughts out of his head like a flock of prattling crows.

"What is the council going to do with the Changeling?" Cary asked Dearth, who had stopped once again to sniff the air, his long snout probing the sky.

"His name is Adarel," Dearth replied. "You should know. You witnessed the punishment."

Cary remembered the statement of punishment made by the council: Adarel would be rendered flightless and imprisoned—all because Cary had pronounced him guilty. Any hope of being a leader in this strange bird-world poured from his heart like sand from a shattered hourglass. His extraordinary, glistening black wings weighed heavily, like a crown for a fool.

"Why do you have to hand me over to the birds?" asked Cary. "Why don't you take me to Husgard Hellir yourself?"

"Too far, too much time—too high," Dearth said, his snout resolutely forward. "Ofost and Gren will guide you the rest of the way."

"Who are Ofist and Gren?"

"Gildenhyrn," answered Dearth. "Ofahst and Gren carried your brother and sister to the safety of Husgard. Vaskar, their captain, was not so fortunate."

"What happened to him?"

"He was attacked by a clutch of old Scarecrow's guards, the Dreygar. You have seen one. He came forward as a witness at Adarel's trial. You had better hope we do not meet a pair of those. Dreygar do not bear the name of "Bloodwing" without merit. They have taken Vaskar captive. I have not found him—or his captors yet."

Dearth finished with a low growl, involuntarily baring

his teeth, which made Cary believe the rodent could be capable of inflicting great harm.

"How much farther?" Cary was tired. He did not want to meet Gren and Ofost. They were sure to blame him for Vaskar's captivity, on top of everything else.

Dearth stopped. "We must cross the Soltin Myrr, easy for a rat, difficult for a..." Dearth strode ahead. "It is a bog with an appetite for foolish boys!"

In another hour, Dearth had stretched his lead, stopping only to motion for Cary to move faster. Cary breathlessly tried to keep up as wafts of damp rotted air assaulted his nose with increasing frequency. Finally, Dearth stopped among a line of trees that ended as if bordering a meadow, but beyond was no field of wildflowers and sweet-smelling grass. When Cary caught up, Dearth stood transfixed by a fog that had shrouded the long grey trunks of dead trees.

At the bottom of an embankment, and to either side, mounds topped with tufts of grass studded the stagnant pools of dark water like small islands. Dearth sniffed the air. The short grey fur wrinkled from his nose to his long keen eyes.

"This is Soltin Myrr," said Dearth. "Keep your wings tight and follow closely. Whisper, and only if you must; enemies watch this bog."

Cary followed Dearth down an embankment to the silent, gloomy bog. In the passing of the next few minutes, the comfort of the forest's verdant trees was swallowed in heavy fog. The long, tilted dead trees stretched up like thin grey ghosts frozen in dramatic poses, their ghostly arms reaching up, pleading to the dull blue haze for relief.

Cary watched Dearth leap into the eerie bailiwick of

ghosts. Cary had to jump from mound to mound, following carefully in the steps of his guide. Once, Cary lost his footing and grabbed the only branch available, Dearth's tail, extracting yet another of the many hisses Dearth had showered on him since leaving Vangorfold. Drops of sweat rolled down Cary's forehead into his stinging eyes and off the end of his nose and chin.

"I have to stop," Cary whispered ahead to Dearth. "I need to rest. It's hard to breathe."

Dearth stopped, surprisingly. Without a word, he turned and sat upright on a mound just ahead of Cary, his tail curled around the thin grey arm of a tree for balance. He reached back into a grey satchel and pulled out another root, broke it and handed a piece to Cary. It tasted like raw potato. They sat in silence, eating, the silent dead trees brooding over them. Cary wiped the sweat off from his brow and away from his stinging eyes. His breathing slowed.

Dearth popped the last bit of root into his long mouth, straightened up and jumped to the next clod of grass. "Keep close."

Cary got up, checked his wings and followed.

They went on for some time, repeating the same step-step-jump over and over again. Dearth leaped easily enough, front paws first, back legs following. For Cary it was more difficult. Two steps on a mound—some spongier than others—before a leap to the next with arms ready to grab a low, sturdy branch to keep himself from plunging into one of the smelly, oily pools. More often than not, Cary's wings snagged a branch; it was like jumping between branches with a half-open umbrella.

Cary leaped from mound to mound. He had lost count

of how many small pools he had avoided. Dearth had moved so far ahead, he was drifting in and out of the grey mist like a phantom.

Cary took two quick jumps, trying to catch up. On his third, his left wing caught a branch, which turned him in the air. He hit the next mound backward on his heels and fell straight onto his back, the back of his head and tops of his folded wings dipped in the foul-smelling ink. Hands gripping some small, short tuffs of grass, Cary held tight, as rigid as a log. High above him, like a sinkhole in the fog, at the highest point of a long silvery trunk, its top bare branches shrouded in a grey haze, loomed a long dark shadow.

Dearth had already returned. "Stand up and keep moving," he hissed.

Cary stabbed his finger in the direction of the dark shape. Dearth followed his prompt.

"How long have you seen those in the tops of the trees?" whispered Dearth, irritated that he hadn't spotted the trouble himself.

"It's the first one," Cary whispered back. "What is it?"

In a second, Dearth slipped a slingshot from his satchel and quickly set a stone in its pocket. In a quick snap he launched the stone at the dark formless shadow. The dark shape suddenly spread large shadowy wings and melted away into the mist.

"Vultori—old Scarecrow's eyes, Scarecrow's claws!" said Dearth. "The spies usually hunt in pairs, so one has flown for help. We have got to move quickly!" He changed direction and moved faster over the mounds. The distance between him and Cary was growing.

Soon the dead trees were replaced by living ones on

larger patches of dry land between pools. Cary could now step and jump easily.

Suddenly, Cary felt a shadow pass overhead. It fell upon Dearth, who turned in an instant to meet his attacker: a Dreygar warrior. The Vultori had summoned help. The nimble rat reached behind his head with both arms and drew out two identical blades. He threw one and hit its mark! The other tapered blade he swept across the open talon of the second Dreygar, who had attacked from behind. The bird of prey sprang away, screeching in pain.

Dearth swung his blade to his left pointing to a column of trees. "Fly! More follow! Fly!" Dearth bounded off in the opposite direction, slashing branches, squeaking like a distressed rat to draw off the Dreygar.

Cary opened his wings. He had managed to lift himself off the ground a couple of times walking behind Dearth, so he tried to repeat the movement. He lifted his wings high and, concentrating on his back, forced down a stroke. It lifted him a foot from the ground. He landed. Another stroke. This time he lifted higher before dropping to touch the mound with an outstretched foot. He flapped harder, tilting his wings, pocketing the air. He was airborne. He found a rhythm and began to beat his wings, jerking himself to the right, recovering to the left, just missing the branches of a several trees. Cary was flying more like a panicked bat than a bird, but he gained momentum, ducking low branches speeding toward him. The ground grew level. He was out of Soltin Myrr.

The crossing of Soltin Myrr had taken too long. It was twilight. Cary could hardly distinguish what lay ahead. He tried to fly low and straight, but with every beat of his wings he almost snagged a dangling foot. Twice he ran and hopped along the ground, wings outstretched like a lame duck hopelessly trying to take off.

Doubtless a pair of claws hung over him ready to grip his back. Still flying, he twisted to defend himself against his imagined attacker. Only mist and trees. But it was a grave mistake. As he spiralled forward, Cary's head and shoulder clipped a wide trunk. He fell in a heap.

He woke up in the dark. Remembering his flight from the Dreygar, Cary immediately stood up and rubbed his forehead and rotated his shoulder. He brushed dirt and leaves off his shirt and pants. Satisfied he had not broken any bones, he instinctively stretched his wings to their full width.

"Impressive."

Cary turned. A large black bird stood not three wing lengths in front of him. The bird's polished blue-black coat glistened under the dim light of the evening sky. The bird was not Harfan, of that Cary could be sure. The bird's beak was larger than Harfan's and curved to a sharper point. A spray of feathers beneath its throat joined a mantle that wrapped its broad shoulders.

"Who are you?" asked Cary, stepping back, ready to fly for his life.

The coal-black bird took a hop forward on its sturdy legs. "A friend."

"You mean you don't belong to Harfan?" asked Cary.

"Harfan? Harfan the crow!" The black bird croaked and rattled deeply. "I belong to no one."

"Can you help me?" asked Cary, not really knowing what to ask next.

"If I can, I will," answered the bird.

"I need to get to Husgard Hellir," said Cary. "Do you

know where it is?"

"Of course," answered the bird. "If Husgard is where you want to go."

"I have to go to Husgard," answered Cary. "I need to meet..." He broke off. He could be offering up too much information too soon. He did not want to mention Dearth, either.

"I can lead you, Ascentor, to where you will find Husgard Hellir," said the bird, its round bright eye fixed upon him like the moon gazing through dark clouds in a midnight sky.

"How do you know I am an Ascentor?" asked Cary.

"I can see many things," said the bird as he lifted his gaze to the canopy of branches above. "But more to the point, how many young Earth-dwellers have you seen flying around the island? I will guide you to where you want to go. But be warned, your new friends may not take lightly to what you have done."

"What do you mean?" asked Cary blankly, suspecting the bird had already gleaned the details concerning Adarel's trial.

"A little advice," said the broad-shouldered bird as it took another hop forward. "Do not banter with an old raven who knows more than you can imagine."

"You mean the Changeling. It's true," conceded Cary. "But I have to go, anyway."

"Understood," said the raven, hopping past Cary, its slate black beak pointing into the wood.

"What about the Dreygar?" asked Cary, thinking his attackers would dart out of the trees at any moment.

The raven clicked and gronked as if it was laughing. "The Dreygar have hobbled back to Vangorfold," said the raven. "Humbled by a rat."

The raven led Cary for the next hour. He said nothing more. He only tilted his broad black beak to the sky once in a while, possibly to confirm his direction.

"Now, if you will permit me, and you are willing, I will teach you a few tricks, young Black Wing," said the raven as it flew off. Cary hesitated only for a moment before he launched from the forest floor and followed the raven as best he could.

The raven was an excellent flyer. His large wings with long, spear-like primary feathers were hardly moving. Cary's breath was shallow and rapid, partly from fear of the height they had reached, and partly because he had been beating his wings many times for every graceful wing sweep of the raven. The raven drifted alongside Cary.

"Spread back your tail feathers. They will give you stability in the turns."

Beyond the tips of his secondaries a fan of long rectangular feathers almost brushed his heels.

"Spread your primaries as if they were your fingers. Stop looking down. Look ahead."

The raven flew just ahead on Cary's left. The raven, like a flight instructor, distinctly adjusted his wings as he demonstrated different manoeuvres. Cary learned how to subtly manipulate a few primary feathers to begin a wide turn, how to pull in both wings to initiate a drop, and, more importantly, to recover.

Like a young bird on its first flight, Cary was adapting quickly. In the next hour, he managed to soar, roll to both sides, climb, and, after a drop, pull up to a full stop. The raven even showed off a little. He flew ahead of Cary and executed an upward full loop that ended in three barrel rolls. Cary was spellbound and smiled at the raven as he did his tricks.

"I'm getting tired," said Cary at last.

He was unmistakably tired, but he was more afraid he might fall if he cramped up or lost the sensation of either of his wings, and the height was making him light-headed. The raven obliged and led Cary down to the edge of a field that shone pale yellow under the moon. They landed in front of the outlying trees of a wood spreading over the foothills of a mountain.

"If you should so choose, young Black Wing," said the raven, "I can teach you much more, but I will need a few turns of the earth and all of your concentration."

After his first official flight lesson, Cary could not resist the invitation. Besides, a little delay in his trip to Husgard might give him time to summon up the courage to face the Changeling's followers.

If seven hours curled in a badger hole cramped Cary's muscles more than he could remember, three full days of flying practice produced a gnawing ache he would never forget in muscles he didn't know he had. On his last morning with the raven, he could not extend a wing without groaning.

"Today you will rest your wings," said the raven, "and exercise your legs. We will walk for a while, fly, and walk again. I shall show you the way to Husgard Hellir."

Cary did not want to go. He had made a friend, and although his sister and brother were waiting for him at Husgard, he could only imagine every other creature there a potential enemy.

"My sister will be worried about me."

"You are right," agreed the raven. "Follow me."

Walking, Cary followed the raven for most of the morning.

"Who are you?" Cary asked, his mouth full of berries. "I mean, I don't know your name."

"My name is Harfan," replied the raven.

"Harfan? Harfan is the leader of Vangorfold."

"Harfan!" the raven squawked. "Harfan is Raven in the old language, but that old impostor on the High Seat at Vangorfold is no raven; he is an old crow who has held power for its own sake far too long. For my sake, then, do not call me Harfan. You may call me Raven Wing."

After Raven Wing answered more questions about the Birdfolc and the island, he struck south for some time along the mountains before he banked left and followed the edge of a forest that bordered a field of long, gold-coloured grass. The raven landed, Cary following suit, and they walked among the trees where they grew farther apart.

"I smell the swamp," said Cary. "It's Soltin Myrr."

"You have not wasted time over your maps," said Raven Wing. "We have returned near to the place we first met." He extended his wing. "The wide expanse before you is the Yellow Fields. Beyond the fields, closer to the sea, is Husgard. From here we must be cautious. We will fly low or walk."

They walked and flew, wherever Raven Wing led. Finally, when the westward sky streaked with pink washes of the setting sun, the raven stopped.

"Fly low over that meadow and through a gap in the trees beyond, and you will reach the sea. Keep the sea on your right wing and fly for the cliffs. Hidden within those high stone walls is the stronghold of Husgard Hellir. If you land among the tall trees at its feet and walk toward the cliff face, those you seek will find you."

Cary turned his attention away from the tree-lined horizon back to Raven Wing.

"It would be better not to mention me," continued Raven Wing. "The Birdfolc of Husgard and Vangorfold, or any other creature of this island, are not friendly toward a raven who has not chosen sides. But I delay. Your opportunity is here, young Black Wing; the moon is veiled."

Cary turned away from Raven Wing to watch the last rim of the moon slip behind a curtain of clouds that had been drawing across it, darkening the landscape that lay ahead. When Cary turned back to thank Raven Wing, he was gone.

CHAPTER FOURTEEN
The Plans of Husgard Hellir

When Dearth finally arrived at Husgard, he was so faint from exhaustion and the poisoned wounds he had received from the Dreygar that he had become delirious. He talked to the Gildenhyrn as if the birds were his own children come to greet him, asking the bewildered warriors if they had behaved well and helped their mother. Dearth had neither children, nor a mate, so many were amused. Later, if the matter were mentioned, Dearth would say, "I talk like a fool after I have been wounded and poisoned. What, pray tell, is your excuse?" The remark would silence all but his peers.

When Cary had not arrived with Dearth, Mandwar immediately sent out scouts in a search, including Ofost, who had returned with Vaskar, and also Gren, who had returned only after searching the area set for the rendezvous.

Vaskar was recovering, slowly. In addition to plucking many of his feathers, his interrogators had beaten him. They did not get a feather of information from Vaskar. The courageous Gildenhyrn, a hero to Birdfolc, would rather have been locked away and forgotten than yield to any of the enemy's demands. Not a bird at Husgard missed inquiring after his health, some on a regular basis.

Clarisse had retreated to her chamber with Gregory, overcome with the news of Dearth's battle with the Dreygar, which left Dearth wounded and Cary lost. Cary was on his own in a strange and dangerous country.

Days later, when news reached Clarisse that Cary had been found wandering the Watcher's Wood near the cliffs of Husgard, she rushed to greet him.

"Cary!" said Clarisse, rushing toward him with Gregory in tow, ignoring the others who had surrounded him. "Are you hurt? How did you find us? You have wings."

"I'm okay," said Cary. "I stayed hidden and walked most of the time. I used the moon to keep me going in the right direction. I got lost once or twice, but it wasn't that bad. All I did at Vangorfold was study maps. They wouldn't let me do much else." He smiled. "You've got wings too."

"I do too," piped in Gregory, who had nudged his way into Cary's view, swiping a couple of Gildenhyrn as he opened his wings to show Cary.

Every creature at Husgard was happy to see Cary reunited with his brother and sister. The Gildenhyrn scouts who had found and escorted the boy could not stop staring. Cary's wings were larger than Clarisse's; in fact, broader than their own and by all appearances more powerful. To Clarisse, Cary's beautiful black wings made his dark hair all the more striking. One of the princely figures she had seen illustrated in her books would have drawn a fitting image.

Clarisse insisted Cary meet Mandwar, if only briefly.

Mandwar had already been observing Cary from a distance and was just as impressed as the others with what he judged to be the wings of a raptor. The dark-winged boy resembled a newly appointed Gildenhyrn, but the owl was puzzled by their brief encounter. Cary did not show fear or any wonder at the luminous caves of Husgard. The young Earth-dweller was extremely tired, yet not hungry. In addition, a four-day journey undercover in the island wilderness, hiding from Dreygar patrols had not left its telltale marks. What was stranger, especially to an owl who wouldn't miss the whisker off a mouse, was Cary's vague description of his adventure. Mandwar politely excused Cary, who rejoined his sister and brother.

After a short tour, the reunited Ascentors retreated to Clarisse's chamber to share their stories. Gregory hardly allowed a sentence to go by without interrupting. Their stories told, at least in part, they wished each other well, said goodnight, and went to bed. Cary collapsed on the nest-bed in his own chamber and fell into a deep sleep.

Dearth roused Cary late the following morning, bearing a tray of food.

"At least you didn't get captured, despite Thumper and Bumper!" Dearth said, laying the tray down on the side of the nest. He had named Cary's wings early on their journey together.

"What about you?" Cary replied, steering attention away from himself. "You had the Dreygar on your tail. I saw you kill the first one."

"Kill? No, I only sent him home with a small token of the cost of trading knives with Fyrndagas Dearth."

Dearth's whiskers were fidgeting as they always did when he was planning or making a decision. "You got lost, made your way across half of Shelter Island, and, in the miraculous manner of an Underdel, found your way to the secret doors of Husgard. Friend, it is you who have been the conversation of Husgard. And on your own. How did you cross the open fields?"

"I flew," answered Cary, "where the field wasn't that wide, across the Vangorian Pass, I think."

"You flew?" asked Dearth, the round beads of his black eyes even rounder. "You must have flown at some height to avoid the Dreygar below and the Vultor spies circling above."

"Actually, I flew very low when I crossed—and walked," Cary answered. "I didn't know what to do, so I headed for the moon."

"The moon? At that time the moon would have led you out to sea," said Dearth.

"That was just part of the way. I flew out over the sea for a ways," Cary paused, trying to recall the compass on the maps he had seen of the island. "North—I kept the moon off my right wing—I was on an island, so it was pretty easy."

"You have studied your maps well, young Ascentor," said Dearth.

He was about to ask another question when, much to Cary's relief, a messenger interrupted.

"Mandwar has summoned us to Folcmot, at once," said the messenger.

"Folcmot?" said Cary

"A meeting—another meeting of too many words. Necessary, but trying!" said a frustrated Dearth, who was much more interested in continuing his conversation with Cary. "Come, Black-Wing of the Moon. You may hide with me at the back."

Cary did not want to answer any more of Dearth's probing questions, but worried he might draw attention to himself if he stayed in his chamber, he followed Dearth to Folcmot.

The messenger led Cary and Dearth down a long passageway and pointed the way through an archway into a cavern at which many leaders from Husgard had already arrived. Birds, and some animals, including a pair of foxes, were perched on flat stones that haphazardly surrounded a larger one, on which stood the owl with the moon-white face. Enthusiastic conversation filled the cavern.

When Cary and Dearth arrived, Mandwar unfurled his impressive wings, silencing the many conversations. An attendant redirected Cary away from Dearth to a large flat rock behind Mandwar, where he joined his brother and sister. Heads turned to follow Cary to his rock perch. As much as possible, Cary avoided the curious gazes cast in his direction.

Mandwar lowered his wings and softly began to sing, not like a bird, more like a human, in a language Cary did not understand. Clarisse told him the words later.

> *Gather folc of Fridorfold*
> *though the horizon dark,*
> *The sun will rise in streams of gold*
> *So sings the meadowlark.*
>
> *Gather folc of Fridorfold*
> *Hope is on the wing.*
> *Humble foot or feather bold*
> *For Fridorfold we sing.*

Gather for Fridorfold, hearts as one!
[all folc present] Hearts as one!
Gather for Fridorfold, hearts all won!
[all folc present] Hearts all won!
Fridorfold!
[all] Fridorfold!

Folcmot commenced. Mandwar first reminded all gathered of the words written in the Song of Fridorfold, reciting some the trials of Birdfolc loyal to Fridorfold from the beginning. Mandwar ended with the same words Gren had spoken to Clarisse when she arrived at Husgard, words set in verse long before:

Three golden feathers found and freed,
Three golden winged bearers to bear the three
Three feather's bearers, then shall lead
On wings born of Fridorfold
As Ascentors three.

Mandwar continued, his left wing extended toward Clarisse, Gregory and Cary. "Our three Ascentors: Arithi, Aevi—and Brador Halar."

Mandwar paused, because Cary's new name in the old Fridorfold tongue literally meant "Hasty Hero," a combination of names that would have sounded very odd to the Husgard folc. Brador was a name often given to young headstrong birds if they were apt to heedlessly hop off into danger. Cary's new name, in contrast to his striking frame, drew curious tilts of the head and wide eyes, though not from the grinning Dearth, who believed the name well suited. "A tail always follows its rat," he whispered to himself.

Mandwar continued, "They have received their wings as the Song foretold. They will join us as leaders in the hope of restoring Fridorfold."

No objection was forwarded, so Mandwar moved on to other business. "Vaskar has been improving steadily since he was rescued by our valiant Gildenhyrn, Ofost and Gren. He sends his greetings and thanks for the overwhelming support he has received. Fyrndagas Dearth, faithful as always, has brought us important information that all present need to hear. Dearth?"

Dearth had already started waving his good arm, his other in a sling, to persuade Mandwar to relay the information himself, but he finally had to yield when all eyes turned to him expectantly.

"If I must," began Dearth. "Adarel, Singer of Ellri, has been tried and found guilty of treason."

Many birds and animals blurted out "How?" or "Why?" Some gasped. Conversations followed. This unexpected straight-to-the-point announcement, typical of Dearth, made Cary afraid of what would follow.

"The traitor Scarecrow, enemy to Husgard, cannot go unpunished for this crime," shouted a Gildenhyrn raptor not unlike Gren. Many voices approved the outburst.

Dearth waited, his eyes on Mandwar, who nodded for Dearth to say what had to be said. Cary was frozen to his cold rock perch.

"It was not Harfan who judged him," Dearth continued. The curious became quiet. Others exchanged whispers repeating his statement. As straight-talking as he was, even Dearth was reluctant to say what had to be said.

"It was not old Scarecrow who passed judgement ... it was our Ascentor, Cary—rather, Brador Halar—who judged in this matter." All went silent.

Why Fyrndagas Dearth said Cary, rather than his Fridorfold name, can only be understood that for the first time since he had met Cary, Dearth felt sorry for adding to the boy's troubles.

Dearth continued, "Harfan orchestrated the trial and deceived the boy—I mean Cary—or Brador Halar," he added. "Three witnesses testified against Adarel, all under the wing of old Scarecrow. None came to his defence."

"One did." It was Cary who had spoken. "Fyrndagas Underdel Dearth broke into the trial to defend Adarel, but I didn't listen to him. I..."

Cary sat down. Every eye of every creature was upon him, except Dearth and Mandwar, who were silently enquiring one to the other for a hint how to proceed. An Ascentor, an Earth-dweller, had tried and convicted Adarel of treason. Adarel was a Singer of Ellri, the one who had summoned the Ascentors in the first place. A thing like this had never happened; it was unthinkable.

Not one of the folc dared say it, but they regarded the black-winged creature that had come to Husgard as an omen of dark things to come, a reminder of how in times past, Earth-dwellers had forsaken Fridorfold and hunted Birdfolc as meat for their tables or corpses to feed the ground. Cary could only follow the mineral veins embedded in the floor and wait for the meeting to finish.

Mandwar guided the meeting to other decisions, other news that needed attention. From time to time, Cary could feel Clarisse's gaze upon him, which made him wonder what she was thinking. Cary decided that she too, like the other creatures present, thought all the worse of him for what he had done. Finally, Folcmot drew to a close. The meeting was adjourned.

Without delay, Cary sought the refuge of his own chamber. Dearth approached Cary but was stopped by Mandwar.

"Give him time," Mandwar urged Dearth.

"Time?" responded Dearth. "It is time passing that we do not have."

"Tell me what you saw beneath the stronghold of Vangorfold," said Mandwar. "Your first report is troubling to me."

"See? Smelled. It was our Ascentor who laid eyes on it—a serpent, at least five of your wingspans long, thick as a tree from the Watcher's Wood, and black—with rings, rings of fire, Cary said, casting a dull orange light. Its head was large, which means it carries a big bite—and let's not forget its wings. The only consolation was its chains."

"Chains can be loosed easily enough," Mandwar said. "No, I have a greater concern. Over so many times passing and turns of the earth, the possibility had not occurred to me. The serpent is a beast we have seen before, in a time past, one we believed destroyed."

Mandwar continued as if thinking aloud, "But why would Blodcroew have the very serpent he conjured burned to ash?"

"Mandwar," Dearth interrupted. "You're rambling—again. What are you talking about? Conjured what?"

"The serpent, the giant snake Brador Halar saw in the dungeons of Vangorfold—if I am not mistaken and..."

"You rarely are," put in Dearth.

"Fyrndagas Underdel Dearth, Guardian and Protector

of Husgard, let me be plain. That was no overgrown snake chasing you through the dungeons of Vangorfold; it was Wyrm."

"Wyrm? The vile serpent is dead—its creator vanquished."

"For many turns of the earth and times passing, I thought the same. It has been hidden from us. And if Wyrm has been unleashed," continued Mandwar, following the threads of gold on the ceiling of the large chamber, "it follows that Blodcroew has passed into this time on silent wings—when, I cannot be sure."

"And the old Scarecrow is his singing canary, not minding the analogy," said Dearth.

"I do mind," said Mandwar, "but you are right."

"Blodcroew will have been at his old mischief for some time," added Dearth.

"Mischief? Blodcroew hates Land-crawlers and wants to destroy even the memory of Fridorfold. He wants to rule Shelter Island and the Fragile Lands. It is mischief of the worst kind. He does not bear the name Blodcroew for the amusement of young Birdfolc. He was a Singer turned sorcerer and will end his mischief when he is ruler over Shelter Island and we are dead."

Mandwar and Dearth left the meeting chamber, moving deeper into their discussion. Although they debated many possibilities, they could not be sure of anything Blodcroew had already done. They could only generally agree the raven was planning an attack on Husgard, and the attack would be soon. They also agreed that this very night, though untrained in his gift, young Aevi should return to the Dome of Times Passing in hopes of gaining any new information.

CHAPTER FIFTEEN
Two Choices

Though unable to avoid regular meals and a daily flying lesson with his sister and brother, the evenings were Cary's own. Gregory had already become everyone's favourite and was busy making new friends. Even Dearth kept his distance when Cary became as abrupt and prickly as an Underdel himself. Other folc at Husgard, not knowing Cary at all, intimidated by the young Earth-dweller's size and dark wings, and confused why an Ascentor would have convicted Adarel of treason, avoided him altogether. Mandwar was so busy with the upkeep of Husgard and the movements of Vangorfold that the two rarely brushed wings. The arrangement suited Cary perfectly.

On his fifth evening at Husgard, after his evening meal, Cary did not go directly to his chamber; instead, he wandered the galleries and caverns. Like Clarisse and Gregory before him, he was fascinated by the luminous golden threads weaving like branches through every gallery, every cavern and chamber. The golden light flowed through the branches, brightening and fading as if leading both the eye and the heart through the underground passages.

It was one such golden thread that led Cary into a chamber the walls of which were covered with tapestries of every description. Some were almost finished, others just started, but all astoundingly beautiful.

Cary passed from tapestry to tapestry. He stopped in front of one large and round. A bird was at its centre, not pictured in court or leading a battle, but lying on his side, bound, surrounded by hundreds of birds flying out toward the edges.

"Adarel," came a voice from behind Cary.

Startled, Cary turned around, involuntarily opening his black wings. The small swallow shrank back, dropping the silk and other yarns, filaments and fibres that he was carrying into the chamber for the next day's work.

"I'm sorry," said Cary, closing his wings. "They get away from me sometimes."

The young swallow stood blinking at him.

"Can I help you pick up your stuff?" asked Cary, already on his way toward the young bird. He picked up two balls of yarn that had rolled a distance away from the young bird's basket.

"The bird who is bound is Adarel," the swallow repeated.

"Why is he surrounded by so many flying birds?" Cary handed the balls of twisted filament to the young swallow.

"Because he set those folc free."

"How?"

"From old Scarecrow."

"Do you mean Harfan of Vangorfold?" asked Cary to be sure they were talking about the same bird.

"I think so. Is there another Harfan?"

134

"Was Harfan holding the birds ... the Birdfolc in his dungeon?"

"No, for many years these folc lived in the territories of Vangorfold. They were afraid of Harfan and tried to escape, but they were caught. Many had young ones and eggs. Old Scarecrow kept all folc who tried to escape under close watch somewhere in Vangorfen."

"Did Adarel rescue them?"

"No—I mean—yes." The young swallow found the word it sought. "He traded himself."

"Do you mean Adarel gave himself up to Harfan so the captured birds could come here, as an exchange?"

"Yes," answered the relieved sparrow, "an exchange."

His answer stung Cary. How could someone who had given himself up for others be guilty of treason? Cary did not have an answer. He stepped back from the young swallow, unable to talk. He turned and walked back to the tapestries to hide his face from the swallow.

The young bird, trying to be helpful, followed Cary to the tapestries.

"That one is you. Only the top of your head has been woven. But you are flying with Vaskar."

The young bird continued his description as Cary moved toward the passageway entrance.

"I'm sorry. I have to go."

Cary backed away from the swallow.

"I'm sorry," repeated Cary. He turned his back to the young apprentice and ducked out of the chamber.

Left down the corridor the passage would lead him to more populated areas of Husgard. He turned right. A few turns and sharp inclines led him to little-used passageways higher in the cliffs.

At the end of a series of ascending tunnels, Cary came to a roughly cut stairway. He caught a draught of cool air. He followed the currents up the steps as if he were following a stream. The narrow passageway grew darker. The luminous golden veins had thinned to threads like the outer branches of a tree. The lower ceiling brushed against the tops of his folded wings.

At the top, Cary had to force his way through a tangle of roots. Wherever he was, it had not been used in a long time.

"Just the place," Cary grunted, freeing a snagged wing.

When he finally wrestled his way through some brambles, stopping again to free his wings, he came out on a flat stone with a wall of rock, a wing's breadth away, on either side. He was on a ledge, a stoop that had been carved out of the side of the cliff, which towered above him. As high as he had come, he had not yet reached the crest of the Husgard cliffs.

The wind caressed his face in cool wisps. He stepped forward and leaned over the edge. He was a step away from a heart-stopping fall to the dark, craggy bottom. He stepped back from the dizzying drop. Cary lifted his gaze to the soft white clouds drifting through the night sky. Off to his left, the silver-white moon paved a brilliant sparkling path over the sea. His heart thumped in his chest like a dull drum.

Cary imagined what it would be like to fly from a ledge such as this. He considered the mechanics of when and how he would open his wings. He began to open and close his wings and move his arms like a diver rehearsing for a competitive dive, but stopped when his thoughts intruded. Even here, so high, so alone, surrounded by beauty, trouble had found him. He had dishonoured himself among those loyal to Husgard and Adarel. Cary stepped a little closer to the edge.

He spread his wings and glared.

"Stupid wings," he said aloud. The glistening black wings made his presence at Husgard unbearable, like someone who wears a team jacket when everyone knows he was cut from the tryouts.

"If I didn't have these wings," Cary said aloud, "no one at Husgard would expect anything from me. This is not my world. I didn't choose to come here, into this mess."

He kept his wings outstretched and scorned them as a despised gift. He would have ripped them off, if he were able, and tossed his burden over the cliff.

The fledgling flyer did not yet know that holding one's wings open on a high ledge, such as this, was an excellent way for a bird to launch.

A surge of wind rushed up the cliff, caught Cary under the open fan of his secondaries and tossed him twenty feet up the cliff's face. The surge swiped him back against the cliff, the force pinning his wings on either side. Before he recovered, the rush of wind vanished. Cary twisted and frantically grabbed at the rock, but his fingertips only slid on the smooth feathers of his flattened wings spread out behind him. He slipped a few feet, bumped on an outcrop of rock, and fell headlong into the dark.

The wind tore past his ears, his wings floundering behind him as if they were ragged props wired on his back. But they were open. Cary flexed and tightened his flying muscles. His wings responded. He caught air like a kite, the sudden change in direction flipping his head forward and back like a rag doll. He had pulled out of the fall.

He steadily beat his wings to stabilize his flight, found an updraft and opened his wings to soar in a wide circular climb. He had fought the sky and won. Now he had to tame his wildly beating heart.

Cary took a deep breath. He stretched his wings and opened his primaries to gauge the changes in the draft. Soaring high above the cliffs, his troubles far beneath him, why return? He could fly away. He had been offered a strange chance, an opportunity that understood his heart better than Cary himself. He would not have to avert his eyes or lower his head sneaking around the passageways of Husgard. He had his wings.

The next morning Dearth rose early to call on Cary, determined to help him. Cary had not slept in his bed. After some inquiry, Dearth picked up Cary's scent leading from the Story Chamber. Dearth stepped out onto the ledge that Cary had discovered the night before. At the back of the ledge, the colour of Cary's hair, lay a single dark feather.

CHAPTER SIXTEEN
A Strange Meeting

Cary would have flown home had he known the way. He believed that once he returned home, once he set foot in the real world, this Birdfolc world would vanish, that the same strange fog that brought him would swallow everything. But how would he get home? To cross the Mirror Sea with no land in sight was too risky, especially if what he had learned about the sea were true. It would have tricked him, like a mirage, into flying in circles until he dropped exhausted into the sea. Inland, the Dreygar would spot him, even if he hid in the swamp. The Veil, if he could find it, was impassable.

It would tear me to shreds, thought Cary.

Dead tired from hours of flying, he flew back to the island. He found a high bluff spiked with a few scraggly pines. He had come to the Far Fells, a territory of the island recorded on his maps as deserted and seldom patrolled.

Silhouetted against the fading night sky, his long black wings folded neatly behind, the bend of his wing extending an arm's length above his head, Cary perched like a brooding winged gargoyle on a cathedral, only less fierce. All this young gargoyle was thinking about was home.

"If you are hoping to cross the sea, I can tell you it does not end, young Black Wing."

Cary almost jumped from the edge of the bluff. It was Raven Wing.

"The Mirror Sea," continued Raven Wing, "however far or long you fly, will lead you back to the island. This island has its rules—rules that can be broken, of course, under the right circumstances, but rules nevertheless."

Raven Wing stopped talking and weighed Cary. "I think your wings have grown since we last met."

"How did you know I was here?" Cary asked, still settling his heart.

"When you fly in front of the moon, as you have been doing for the last hour, it was not difficult," replied Raven Wing.

The lamp of the moon. He had made himself clearly visible. Raven Wing was right.

"You are new to the island," said Raven Wing.

"Rules? What rules?" returned Cary, wanting to deflect attention away from his novice mistake.

"Rules that govern our worlds, the laws of the Lost Veil, of times passing and the laws of the Ellri. There are others."

"At least where I come from, you know the rules before you decide to play the game," Cary snapped back.

"True enough. However, even in your world you play some games not knowing the rules before you start. You learn the rules as you play."

Cary did not respond, so Raven Wing continued. "For example, growing up, or getting along with your sister and brother, or standing up to the young man who smacks you on the back every now and again."

"How did you know that?" interrupted Cary.

"Do you think the Fragile Lands is home only to Earth-dwellers?"

"It doesn't matter; I get your point," said Cary. "So what are the rules I need to know to get..."

"Home?" asked the raven.

Cary did not respond. Raven Wing, who had twice extended a wing when he needed help most, was the first bird in this world, or first creature from any world that had not forced him to do something; on the contrary, the raven had taught him flying manoeuvres that had saved his life only a few hours before.

Raven Wing walked past Cary, closer to the edge of the bluff, and gazed out over the sea. Cary compared the raven's wings with his own.

"The turning of the Earth and the Fragile Lands are the first rules. You are now on an island behind the Lost Veil, a place between times passing. The island shares many of its laws with the turning of the Earth, but as an island it has its own laws. The Realm of Ellri sees all things. All three are bound, but in different times passing. When you passed through the Veil, you passed out of time and out of reach of the Fragile Lands. What I can tell you is this: you must return through the Lost Veil to get home."

"How do I do that?" he asked.

"You? You cannot. You must be borne hence by one who can. But you have grown large, much too large to carry."

Cary remembered his ride on the shoulders of Vaskar of the Gildenhyrn, but Vaskar was at Husgard, along with Mandwar and everyone else he had fled. None of the Gildenhyrn would be permitted to guide him back.

"There is, however, another way," said Raven Wing, as if finishing Cary's thought. "The Lost Veil did not always exist; it was created by one among the Ellri."

"Why?" asked Cary.

"To separate Birdfolc from Earth-dwellers; to exile Birdfolc to this island. Birdfolc are no longer free to visit the Earth at will—the law of the Ellri. You have met one. At Husgard Hellir, he is named Adarel."

Cary winced at the hearing of Adarel, at how he had condemned the courageous bird.

"Do not worry," said the Raven. "He must remain our captive, but will be treated much like you were when you first arrived at Vangorfold. It is believed that Adarel created the veil, which is why he must remain our captive. As long as he is our captive, the Veil weakens."

Raven Wing finished. He and Cary stood for a moment, the sea breezes washing over them, tustling their feathers. Cary's shoulders were heavy with the growing weight of his new wings. Instead of flying to freedom, he felt as if he had escaped a cave to get trapped in a cage.

"Till you are able to pass through the Veil, as an Ascentor, you are leader of Vangorfold, if you should choose it."

"Harfan is leader of Vangorfold," objected Cary. "And he has a giant snake hidden in his dungeon. My sister and brother are at Husgard. If I go back to Vangorfold, I'll be an enemy to Husgard. I'm not going to fight against Clarisse and Gregory."

"Harfan? The old crow has left Vangorfold, along with his pet."

"How?" asked Cary, surprised.

"He has agreed that the law and the signs stand, that the Ascentor should rule in his stead—without his meddling.

You can help bring freedom to every creature trapped on this island, as it was in times past. The Veil is fading. In a short time the exiles can return. There will be no need to fight against your brother and sister. With the veil destroyed, you, along with your brother and sister, will fly home. Adarel will be freed."

"What can I do?" asked Cary. "I'm already in trouble."

"Do? Not do, but are. You are an Ascentor. You will have a newly appointed council of your own choosing. You will have me. We will hold Adarel and we will wait."

Cary remembered what Raven Wing had said about Birdfolc on the island not being friendly toward his kind.

"Which side are you on?"

"I am on neither side," answered Raven Wing. "I am of the ancient world. I am on the side of the world that was once shared by Earth-dwellers and Birdfolc. I am on the side of freedom. Harfan, as the crow calls himself, ruled the folc of Vangorfold with the beating wings of fear, which is why he kept the serpent in his dungeon. Harfan and Mandwar cannot see beyond this island, a realm both desire to rule. Vangorfold and Husgard have been locked claw in claw in this struggle for many times past. Harfan's seat sits empty. Time to leave the nest, young Ascentor Black Wing."

Cary shook his head in doubt.

"The Veil is fading. Who better than you, a winged Ascentor, to lead us to the Fragile Lands and unite Birdfolc and Earth-dwellers." Raven Wing turned to face the first rays of the rising sun.

"The day is upon us, Ascentor Black Wing. Choose your path."

CHAPTER SEVENTEEN

What Gregory Saw

It was agreed upon at once, with his permission of course, that Dearth should return to Vangorfold Stronghold to watch for any unusual activity or any news of Cary.

No news from fur or feather of Cary had arrived since his flight from Husgard. Clarisse, who could predict Cary's reactions better than anyone, believed he would return if given a little time.

"Time is the treasure of which we are poorest!" was all Mandwar said before taking counsel with himself under the Dome of Times Passing.

"Where did Cary go?" asked Gregory, stuffing his mouth full of his favourite berries.

"If you keep eating berries like that, you're going to get sick," warned Clarisse, "or turn into a bird."

"I am a bird!" replied Gregory in a muffled voice.

Like Gregory, Clarisse's appetite had grown in proportion to her wings. To her embarrassment, she was eating twice as much as she usually did at evening table. She told

Gregory that the person who had come up with the saying, eating like a bird, to describe a small appetite, did not know what they were talking about. It must have been the flight practice that she and Gregory were undertaking in the caverns of Husgard, or the endless walking through Husgard's passageways that had carved out such a cavernous appetite.

"At least you can save some for me," chided Clarisse, chasing Gregory around her chamber.

After wrestling a few berries from Gregory before he could stuff the last of the sweet treats into his mouth, Clarisse sat with him on the edge of her nest-bed.

"You didn't answer me. Where did Cary go?"

"I don't know," answered Clarisse.

"Why did he leave?"

"I'm not sure."

"Is he in trouble?" Gregory was thinking that Cary might have done something to get himself into trouble in the same way he had often done.

"No."

"Is he flying?"

"I don't know."

"Is he coming back?"

Gregory's simple question betrayed the thought that had been growing inside her without her knowing.

"I don't know," she said heavily.

"Let's go and look for him," said Gregory, standing up. "We can fly."

"But we don't know the island well enough, where to hide, the best routes. We could get lost, and that would only make everything worse. Better to wait with the others until we're called."

"But I want to do something."

"Come and watch me practice my archery. If you behave and stop fidgeting, maybe I'll let you shoot an arrow or two."

Archery was one of the principal skills among the Gildenhyrn, who were very pleased to discover Clarisse had some knowledge of the skill. Appointed as an Ascentor, she had been supplied with the most exquisite bow and the supplest, well-feathered arrows she had ever seen. If ever there were a marked improvement because of having the right tools, this was such an occasion. Clarisse was accurate at home; here, she rarely missed her mark. Her wings had stablized her balance, and the excellent arrows flew truer than any she had nocked to a bow string.

The arrows were footed arrows, each shaft with its distinct grain of wood. The fletches or stabilizing feathers were flawless, as Clarisse expected from Birdfolc, who would certainly know their trailing vanes from their leading vanes.

As well as being able to hit a very small target, Clarisse—more often called Arithi now—had proven to be very capable in making smart and brave choices, as her namesake had done long ago. She had been present when Mandwar and Dearth were discussing Cary's flight from Husgard. It had been her suggestion that Mandwar post archers, including her, along the northwest edge of Arafen to watch and wait. If Cary were to return from the Golden Fields or the Far Fells, he would have to cross the Freewind. And Arithi, like Mandwar, had read the uneasy, troubled winds blowing from the south in the same way the citizens of the Fragile Lands predicted a storm before it hit the continent.

Mandwar had his own troubles brewing in his mind. He needed information. What was the old Scarecrow planning? Why had the sky been emptied of Vultori and the Dreygar? Where had Cary gone? More importantly, what punishment had the old crow meted out upon Adarel? Mandwar had to resist the urge to do something simply to relieve the worry of not knowing. He had to watch and listen, and he would begin with Gregory.

When Mandwar and Gregory entered the Dome of Times Passing that evening, the golden branches adorning the top of the dome were as bright as Mandwar remembered. Gregory eagerly walked under the canopy to gaze into its branches.

"The branches are sparkling," he said.

"They are indeed," agreed Mandwar. "When you are ready, look between the branches as you did before."

Gregory concentrated his gaze on the spaces between the golden branches. The branches started to fade from their brilliance as the spaces between turned deep blue. One by one from the top, stars sparked to life, as they had done when Gregory first gazed up into the dome, drawing his gaze down the side of the canopy into a panorama of mountains. On one side, the mountains grew larger. Two peaks loomed ahead but shifted to each side as if Gregory were passing between their long slopes. In a moment, the mountain peaks moved to the opposite side of the dome and were now behind him. He returned his gaze to where the mountain peaks appeared...

"I don't see anything," he said. "The mountains are gone. I'm going fast—through clouds."

"You have passed over the Muna Mountains, bordering the Golden Fields to the west," said Mandwar. "Look ahead—to the mists—the Lost Veil. You are passing through the Veil. Do you see the Fragile Lands?"

"No ... fog ... blowing really fast."

"You are passing through time and space, Aevi. Keep watching."

"The fog's gone. I am flying down, really fast. I'm over a field ... There's a forest. I can see the trees now—very close. I'm not flying anymore."

"Hold your gaze, Aevi," said Mandwar. "Look around you. Tell me what you see."

The trees surrounded him. Three quarters of the way round the dome, a long shaft of light broke through an opening between long trunks, possibly leading to the field he had just seen. A dark shape emerged.

"I see something," said Gregory. "A bird—a big black bird talking to a tree. No wait—the bird's talking to someone behind the tree."

As if he were walking in the wood itself, Gregory moved closer to the side of the dome, closer to what was behind the tree. Suddenly, he cried out. He was so startled, he tripped over his own wings and fell backward. The scene between the golden branches returned to stone. In one hop, Mandwar was over Gregory, his wings wrapped around him like a hen over her chick.

"I'm sorry," said Mandwar to Gregory, who was trying to catch his breath. "It was too much—too soon. Catch your breath."

"It was a snake—a giant snake," said Gregory between breaths. "When I yelled, the big black bird—the bird that was talking to it, turned—he looked at me. He saw me."

"Likely not," said Mandwar. "Felt you, possibly, like a breath from the shadows. Aevi, the bird and the snake were on the earth in some time past, and you are here, in the present, under the wing of a big grumpy owl with a bad temper if anything should threaten his young ones. Brave Aevi, you have seen something of utmost importance. Come with me. We are going to the Story Chamber."

"I like that place," said Gregory, already settling down.

"I want you to tell the Story Weavers what you have seen. I will send Clarisse to meet you—with treats!"

By the time Gregory had found his way to the Story Chamber, Clarisse had already arrived. Gregory had been thinking mostly of the treats.

It took a lot of coaxing and many berries to draw out the details the weavers needed for the tapestry. When the weavers had sufficient details, Gregory and his sister went back to Clarisse's chamber, but not before Clarisse investigated every corner. Gregory thought that the snake might have seen him and was hunting him.

What Gregory had seen did not frighten Mandwar, but did puzzle him. The snake was possibly the same beast that had chased Dearth and Cary under Vangorfold. But it was a wonder to Mandwar the serpent had been somewhere on the Fragile Lands in a time past.

Later, Gregory described the large black bird in more detail for Mandwar. He used his hands to shape the black bird's overlarge shoulders, as if its shoulders were wrapped in a fur mantle. He described the bird's beard-like spray of black and grey feathers under its throat, round piercing eyes, and a wide wingspan that revealed a long black sword, the same sword the black bird had held under the snake's gullet. One bird matched Aevi's description: Blodcroew.

CHAPTER EIGHTEEN

Bracing for the Worst

Mandwar was convinced Blodcroew was hatching a long-laid plan to seize Shelter Island, but why the raven had risked a trip to the Fragile Lands, why and how he had resurrected the ancient Wyrm, he could not answer.

Another message was delivered to Mandwar, more disturbing than the revelation of Blodcroew's return. Mandwar learned that in the absence of Harfan, the young Ascentor, Brador Halar, had forsaken Husgard, carrying many of its secrets, and assumed the High Seat of Vangorfold—the very throne the young man had recently escaped. The wind had indeed changed; a dark storm was gathering.

News of Cary reached Clarisse, who had assumed her post with the other archers along the border of Arafen.

What has Cary done? she thought. Getting caught up in a Vangorfold conspiracy to imprison Adarel was one thing, but to betray Husgard and his own sister and brother? How had this strange world separated her from her brother?

Arguing over Gregory shrivelled to a very small frustration compared to the events unfolding in this new world.

After Clarisse was relieved from her shift watching the Golden Fields, Mandwar met her at the safe haven of Husgard with an apology. He was sorry he had been so blind—"A very bad thing for an owl," he said—to not recognize how Cary must have felt, arriving at Husgard only to declare that on his first day as an Ascentor, he had been responsible for Adarel's imprisonment. Mandwar remembered how Cary had avoided every creature within Husgard's caves. "A better owl would have intervened," Mandwar said.

Far away, past the swamps of Soltin Myrr, beyond the closely watched Vangorfen Forest, Dearth had unsuccessfully made one attempt to enter the Vangorfold Stronghold. His secret entry points had been blocked up. Its base was so heavily guarded, Dearth imagined that if the birds guarding the stronghold had all extended their wings, they would have formed an unbroken circle around its trunk. Dearth's return had been anticipated.

Restless, hidden out of range of hearing or seeing anything of value, Dearth bound off in search of Harfan, mumbling, "Trouble always has a tail." The stealthy Husgard spy quickly passed through Vangorfen, following his nose, sniffing for the faintest whiff of old crow.

Close by, unaware of Dearth's attempt to enter the stronghold, Cary had been watching for the return of Raven Wing, who had assured Cary he was beginning preparations for the reuniting of the two worlds.

Cary was chairing a formal gathering of counsellors when he was interrupted by a messenger. The same fierce bird that Cary had seen relaying a message to Harfan had landed on the sill of the porthole entry to the Council Chamber. He was a scout. He had urgent news for the Ascentor. Cary walked with the bird to a smaller adjoining chamber.

The armoured bird bowed.

"I have report that Husgard is grouping its warriors and has posted archers along the Freewind. Yellow-wings have been spotted high over our territory. Animals and Yellow-wings have been meeting in the Watcher's Wood, northeast by the sea. Husgard is planning an attack on Vangorfold."

"Why?" asked Cary, crestfallen he had to face bad news so soon. Raven Wing had said there would be no fighting.

"Ascentor, permit me to say—you have one of their leaders, the Changeling, captive. They will try to free him at any cost and crush Vangorfold at the same time, if they can."

Cary dismissed the scout. Not wanting to repeat his mistake of making a decision on his own, he rejoined the council to relay the message. The council was unanimous. A defence should be mounted at once.

With hundreds of Birdfolc families under Cary's wing, he had no choice but to agree and wait for the return of Raven Wing.

Dearth quickly discovered that Harfan, along with his councillors and a large contingent of fighting Dreygar, had not lingered in the southwest. A porcupine who was no friend of Vangorfold had seen a large flock following the

Muna Mountains north. At the Vulton Crags, home to the Vultori, Dearth discovered that Harfan had organized an army, its numbers being added to every hour.

On his treacherous return to Husgard, the stealthy rat found the southern border of the Golden Fields heavily guarded. Squads of birds were positioned along the Fridorian Pass. By all accounts, Dearth's report had confirmed what Mandwar suspected; Vangorfold was preparing to lay siege to Husgard.

CHAPTER NINETEEN

Carey's Flight

In the days that followed, the Council Chamber at Vangorfold Stronghold was converted into a command post, the larger table now covered with maps. Scouts were continuously delivering reports. Cary was thankful the intelligence was simply a confirmation of which they had already prepared. Husgard had mobilized its forces.

The Watcher's Wood, a strategic high point both to the sea and inland, was controlled by the Gildenhyrn, a force that could not be challenged without provoking a battle on a much larger scale. The lines had been drawn.

It was as if Cary were playing a chess game, but much more serious, the moving pieces risking real lives. To his relief, two scouts reported that the defences were in place. However, it was left to Cary to approve of any future movements of the force. Planning a battle was one thing; taking charge over a battle was another.

Before dropping exhausted into his nest-bed, Cary had been regularly flying in the late evenings, partly for the fresh sea air but mainly to get away from the stress of the war room. The Council Chamber was connected to a smaller chamber leading to an outdoor platform that overlooked the sea. It proved an excellent stoop from which to launch.

With every flight, Cary flew higher, testing his wings out of sight of any curious sentries. He practiced flying manouevres until he could do the most difficult without thinking. He could collapse into a roll in either direction and swoop up to a full stall before piking into a tight dive. He executed barrel rolls, and more importantly, he learned how to keep his wings out of range of his sword.

Cary hoped Raven Wing, who had been a good teacher, would return soon, not only for more flying lessons, but to take over the defence of Vangorfold. There had not been one report of his return.

One evening Cary decided to practice soaring, a skill that required all his concentration to prevent his legs from dangling down like a wasp's.

From his lofty vantage point, the northern reaches of the Golden Fields glowed a dull yellow under the moonlight. Steam rose from Soltin Myrr as from a black cauldron. Cary turned his gaze west to the Muna Mountains. Some distance away, a bird darted across his flight path. Birdfolc were not permitted to fly at night. Cary guessed the bird might be carrying information about Husgard, or was a spy, so he gave chase.

Cary quickly shortened the gap, but the moment he drew close to his quarry, the bird barrel-rolled and dropped out of sight. Cary rolled off in pursuit. The bird had vanished.

After a short search, Cary turned back to the root tower. The same bird looped up in front of him again, this time flying away from him, toward the sea. Cary doubled his effort to overtake the trickster. He drew close. Luminescent markings spotted and striped its feathers. Suddenly it barrel rolled and blended into the night sky.

"Ugh!" groaned Cary. "No more playing cat and mouse."

"A trick I am sure you would like to know," said a voice from behind.

Cary rolled onto his back, spread his wings, and pulled up to face his challenger, his sword drawn.

A wing flashed in front of Cary, knocking the sword from his hand. Cary watched helplessly as the sword fell, its blade catching flashes of the moon as it flipped and spun like the needle of a crazy compass before it was cloaked in mist. His only weapon was gone.

"You will not need the sword," said the voice, again behind Cary.

Cary turned to face his attacker. Tangled in his own wings, Cary dropped but recovered quickly and fled for the stronghold.

"I have no wish to harm you," said the voice off his left wing.

A length or two off Cary's left wing soared a bird of his own size, its colours fading in and out as if its feathers were the surface of rippling water.

"We need your help," said the bird.

"We?" challenged Cary. "Who are you?"

"I am Adarel."

It was the Changeling, the bird he had sent to prison. But this bird was bigger than Cary remembered.

"Adarel? Adarel is in prison. I put him there. Who are you?"

"You did not imprison me; Harfan did. He deceived

you into doing what he had always intended. Have you so soon forgotten the tapestry that records plainly how I delivered myself to Harfan in exchange for prisoners?"

Cary remembered the tapestry at Husgard. How could this bird have known what was on the tapestry unless he had seen them?

"I bring you this in token." The bird drew closer, almost wingtip to wingtip with Cary. Slipped between the outer primary feathers was a long slender knife. It was Dearth's.

"How did you get that?"

"From Fyrndagas Underdel Dearth, of course. Its companion is now at Vangorfold Stronghold, recently removed from the shoulder of the Dreygar that attacked him."

"But you are in prison," responded Cary.

"Not at present, as you can see," responded Adarel. "I am a firegast, a winged spirit. I will soon return, feather and spirit, to the Realm of Ellri."

"Where is that?" asked Cary.

"I am dying," responded Adarel.

"Dying? Raven Wing said you would be well-treated."

"I am below Vangorfold Stronghold in a dungeon. Harfan shackled me in the dark and left me without guard or rations."

"But you are here. You are free," said Cary.

Cary and Adarel were soaring so high that a greater part of Shelter Island was shrouded under cloud. Except for an air current caressing the tips of their primary feathers, both flyers were motionless, soaring effortlessly, as if time and gravity had been interrupted.

"I will soon fly from this time passing."

"I'll go now and get you out," said Cary.

"Even if my release were possible, you would be too late. The time to pass has come."

Cary and Adarel flew on in silence. In the quiet, Adarel began to sing.

> *Song of the wild,*
> *Breath of the wind,*
> *Sing where comfort calls.*
> *Sing though the shadow falls.*
> *Over lofty mount or hidden vale,*
> *in earthy den or airy nest,*
> *on heavy path or windy trail,*
> *in happy heart or heavy breast,*
> *Sing when comfort calls.*
> *Sing where shadow falls.*

If a breeze or river could sing, it might sound like this song.

This bird is the one I judged, thought Cary. *I am responsible for his death, and he's singing me a song?*

"This is from the first song," said Adarel. "Our folc will need it in the days ahead. Now, you must listen carefully."

As light and peaceful as a spirit himself, Cary flew effortlessly alongside Adarel as the firegast told the story of Shelter Island and the Lost Veil, of Mandwar, Blodcroew, and his crimes and exile, and of Arithi, just as Clarisse had learned the tale from Gren.

"I am on the wrong side," Cary suddenly blurted out. "Raven Wing has placed me on the throne of Vangorfold."

"Raven Wing did not put you on the High Seat. You chose it when it was offered. Nevertheless, you are on the right side, the side of all folc, the side of Fridorfold."

"Who is Raven Wing?" asked Cary. "He told me he was on neither side, that he was from the old world. He said he wanted to set us free, to reunite Earth-dwellers and Birdfolc. He said he would get us home."

Adarel glided a distance away, drifting farther away with every one of Cary's wing beats.

"I am passing to the realm of Ellri."

"Who is Raven Wing?" asked Cary, louder. He banked to move closer to Adarel, but Adarel distanced himself even more. He was fading.

Before he called out again, a whisper swirled into his ear, as if Adarel were inches away, "You will know Raven Wing when the Song rises in the wind."

Adarel was gone. Cary flew a short distance in each direction of the compass, but instead of finding Adarel, he ended up a short stone's drop above Vangorfold Stronghold. In the east, the clouds were dusted with hints of the rising sun. Cary had flown beside Adarel the entire night.

CHAPTER TWENTY

Raven Wing

Mandwar received troubling news from the Fragile Lands. A strange disease was spreading among Earth-dwellers, leaving young and old deathly sick in its wake. Suspicions had arisen that the disease had come from a point in one of its longest rivers.

Dearth, who had disliked flying under any circumstances, was dispatched between two strong Gildenhyrn to wherever his keen eye and rat sense would lead him.

Dearth did not have to search far from where Gregory had seen Blodcroew talking to Wyrm. A giant snake would need an exceptionally roomy lair. In the vicinity of the first town that had reported an outbreak of the disease, in an outcrop of rock on a forested hillside, Dearth found an opening to a cave. The dirt floor at the opening was polished smooth, a sign the entrance had been frequently used by a footless creature. The overpowering reek of snake fouling the partially lit tunnel was unmistakable.

Dearth advanced deeper underground and stepped

into a large vault of rock and shadow. As his eyes adjusted to the dull and dusty light, piles of dirt emerged from the gloom here and there over the vault's floor like burial mounds. He slipped in for a closer examination.

Dearth found not burial mounds but a clutch of long eggs, like enormous white capsules scattered over the sandy floor. On closer inspection, Dearth counted three eggs that had hatched and three trails winding into the shadows.

Of the destination of the serpent's offspring Dearth was certain; the hatchlings had left slick trails exiting through the rear of the vault onto a steep hillside. They trailed across a nearby field, through a wood and slipped into the river. Surely their poisonous slime was the source of the foul plague.

Abandoning the eggs as they lay for fear of a curse upon them, for the first time in Dearth's long life, he allowed his Gildenhyrn escorts to carry him without hesitation, so much was he in haste to return to Shelter Island and to Husgard.

"The conjured snake that laid those cursed eggs," said Dearth, recounting the story to Mandwar, "left a trail leading to a nearby river."

"How do we destroy eggs," wondered Mandwar, "when in their destruction, a worse plague could be released the moment we crack a shell? Blodcroew's sorcery has given birth to a new enemy. He has finally hatched his foul plan. He will conquer Shelter Island, destroy Earth-dwellers from off the Fragile Lands, and rule all folc, fur or feather, from his High Seat at Vangorfold."

"Sorcery is not our only problem," added Dearth. "When we returned, we saw Dreygar and Vultori circling above the Vulton Crags. Battle is in the wind and will soon be over the fields."

Dearth and Mandwar continued in close discussion, Clarisse joining in. Leaders of the Gildenhyrn, foxes and other ground dwelling creatures followed. It was a call to Folcmot, and to battle plans.

Underway at the stronghold of Vangorfold, another important meeting was interrupted when Cary alighted on the sill of the entry portal. Every head turned, including Raven Wing's. He had returned to aid in the defence of Vangorfold. Cary's arrival had broken a tense moment, sparing Cary's councillors and chaperones a sharp rebuke from Raven Wing for letting their Ascentor fly unaccompanied.

"Welcome, Ascentor," said Raven Wing as he nodded. The other birds followed suit. "We trust you have no ill news."

"Just ghosts," said Cary, uneasy about revealing news of his encounter of the night before, his remark drawing amused tilts of the head from the gulls, who did not believe in things they could not scavenge or swallow.

"I've been flying—practicing," continued Cary, "but I dropped my sword."

"If a dropped sword is the only bad news we hear today, it will mean a fortunate day," said Raven Wing. "Come. Join us. There is much for you to know."

Cary spent the remainder of the morning listening to Raven Wing expertly position squadrons and other strike forces.

At the busiest point, Cary withdrew from the table of maps and asked an attendant to check on the Changeling. Cary had planned to free Adarel himself, but his oversized wings made him a spectacle to the many Birdfolc that had been summoned to the stronghold. Beaks and eyes were on him at every height and hollow.

As leader of Vangorfold, Cary's request had drawn no undue attention, other than a raised eye from Raven Wing. But Raven Wing said nothing and continued to confidently assert his defence preparations.

"We are well defended," Raven Wing assured Cary. The leaders of Vangorfold had walked out to the same stoop that Cary had flown from the night before.

"What do we do now?" asked Cary.

"Do? Nothing, for the time being but watch and wait," said Raven Wing. "We do not want to provoke an unnecessary attack, though battle may soon come to us. The Lost Veil has weakened. Shelter Island will soon dot the horizon, visible to the Fragile Lands. Though forgotten, Birdfolc will join Earth-dweller, as in times past."

A sentry hopped onto the stoop behind Cary and Raven Wing. "A message for the Ascentor."

Cary walked to the messenger while Raven Wing traced the horizon at the far reaches of the sea.

"The Changeling is dead," said the messenger. "He died sometime in the night."

Cary made no response but only stared at the messenger. Uncomfortable, the young bird bowed and backed off the stoop.

Raven Wing hopped around. "That fool of a crow, Harfan, must think all birds are scarecrows like himself, needing neither food nor drink. He will pay for his mistake. Our prisoner could have been of much use to us in a parley with Husgard. Unnecessary and unfortunate."

Raven Wing turned. He continued speaking to the sea, but for Cary's ear.

"This is unwanted and unfortunate news," continued the Raven. "However, it does serve our purpose."

"How?" asked Cary, who struggled against the ache rising in his chest. "Won't Mandwar and the others at Husgard come after us?" Forgetting himself, he added, "Adarel was their leader."

At the mention of Adarel's name, a gust of wind blew up, ruffling their feathers. Faintly at first, from out of the wind, ringing clearer with each word, arose a song, the same song Adarel had sung the night before. Raven Wing stood like stone, as if hypnotized by the sea, the gusts of wind tussling his glossy black feathers.

As the last words drifted through Cary's mind, a voice as true as a Robin's trill rang in his hear, "The Song of Fridorfold is upon the wind. Look to the sign."

Raven Wing said nothing throughout the song. The leader's gaze had wandered over the waves, possibly thinking about something else. Maybe the song had slipped by him altogether.

"Did you hear that?" asked Cary. "Did you hear the song?"

Raven Wing swung his black granite beak toward Cary. Cary took a step backward, stunned. The glossy black feathers on his face and neck had turned grey, a few stragglers completely white. Blood had welled up in Raven Wing's eyes.

"Your eyes," said Cary, taken aback at the blood trickling over Blodcroew's lower lid, "...they're bleeding."

Raven Wing raised a wing to his eye. "The price of too many dangerous passages through the Veil, I expect. Do not worry about me. I will tend to this. You think on what is at hand. We will talk again this evening."

Raven Wing brushed by Cary, his one wing held up to cover his eye as he left the stoop, exposing more feathers that had turned white. Cary was left alone.

A shadow of a bird passed over the root wall. Cary twisted around but found only the sea and the horizon beyond. But the words of the song lingered, as if they were floating down to the sea before they dissolved on the waves.

Cary stared out into the deepening blue. The tears of blood—the white feathers; it was the sign, the mark. Adarel had answered Cary's question. Raven Wing was the ancient Blodcroew.

He had befriended a raven older than the island, a sorcerer that could kill him in an instant. Heedless of the dizzying height over the cliffs, Cary stood on the edge of the stoop, the dark entrance to the tower threatening from behind. Blodcroew could return any moment. Cary paced two steps back from the edge. In two strides, his wings poised, he leapt.

CHAPTER TWENTY-ONE
The First Battle

Cary did not fly to Husgard. The leaders of Husgard would certainly blame him for the death of Adarel. And why not? Cary blamed himself for not searching out Adarel in time to save him.

Blodcroew must have wanted Adarel dead as much as Harfan did. Where was the old Scarecrow, anyway? If the two Vangorfold leaders were working together, Harfan must be close.

It doesn't matter, Cary thought. When they get the chance, they'll throw me into a dungeon like Adarel.

Cary recounted the situations in which Blodcroew, if he had chosen to, could have killed him. He had been a fool. The blood rushed from Cary's head. The sea and the horizon blended into a swirling haze. He had to escape. Escape now. But where?

He dared not fly north into Husgard territory or west toward the mountains watched by the Vultori. Even if he managed to cross the mountains unseen, west would lead him to the Great Waste and the impassable Lost Veil. East was the endless Mirror Sea, the apparitions of which tricked wanderers to fly in circles. He had to go somewhere. Now.

He caught a rising current of air that carried him to a great height. Though he had abandoned his troubles far below and not a living creature had tracked him, Cary was trapped. He was tired too, tired of running, tired of fighting off accusing thoughts that flew at his mind like open talons.

He recalled how he had foolishly regarded himself a judge and leader, of how he buried himself in more and more trouble, and worse, how he had deserted Clarisse and been jealous of Gregory. Each person abandoned and every bad decision clung to him like heavy stones slung around his neck. Cary barely found the will to hold his wings to either side.

"I'm sorry," he said aloud. "I'm sorry," he said, again and again.

His eyes ached and blurred. He wept. It was an effort to breathe. A wingspan ahead his flight path was a smear. He was lost, his strength gone, his downcast heart as heavy as a millstone dragging him down. In a moment he would stop resisting altogether, collapse his wings, and drop from the sky.

He swiped his eyes. Not only was his vision blurry; he had wandered into a sullen grey fog.

"Lost." Cary almost snickered. "Perfect."

But the mists had already begun to clear. And he was flying as fast as had ever, without effort, the way he had flown beside Adarel.

Had he flown too high?

But that's impossible, he thought, *I can breathe*. In fact, along with flying, his lungs expanded and contracted without effort. With every sweep of his wings, the sky brightened. Ahead, broad coloured shapes floated into place as if behind a misted window. A landscape formed.

As he continued to soar effortlessly through the last wisps of mist, the sky turned bright blue, like the bluest of skies over a tropical sea. A white strip lay beyond. A beach.

In a moment, Cary was flying low over a tropical, crystalline sea, approaching a white strip of sand bordered by thick vegetation with high mountains rising in the distance. He alighted on the white beach. He had landed beside a wide stream flowing out from the swooping palms. Never, not even in the reference library in Freeton had he seen such a place.

Cary cupped his hands, scooped up some water, and sipped. It was cool and sweet, like coconut milk. He quenched a deep thirst. The white sand stretched to the horizon in both directions. He turned to the sparkling sea.

Far off, a small luminescent dot flared against the backdrop of blue and grey pillowy clouds. The speck widened to a white sliver. A bird was flying toward Cary with greater speed than the raptors of the Gildenhyrn.

Blodcroew's probably completely white by now. Cary measured the distance to the bank of trees behind the beach. *He's coming after me.*

Cary remembered his dream, how he had been dragged along a white beach by a merciless gull. The bird was flying straight at him. Its speed was even greater than Cary had first guessed. He reached for his sword, but it wasn't in its scabbard. He had not grabbed a replacement at Vangorfold. Flying was useless. He could only stand and wait.

Flashes of colour shimmered across its expanding wings.

It can't be Blodcroew, Cary thought, *unless he can change colours.*

A song skimmed over the waves. Flying toward him was a bird he had met before. Adarel alighted on the beach.

"Where am I?" Cary asked.

"You have passed into the Realm of Ellri."

"How?"

"You entered our Realm when you flew through its gates."

"I didn't see any gates," said Cary, puzzled.

"The gates are hidden but are, at times, revealed when folc have nowhere else to turn. You have passed into the Song; the Song into you."

"I didn't hear a song," said Cary, "at least—not when I was over the Mirror Sea."

"Your sorrow has not followed you here," said Adarel.

"But it's just a beach. Where is everyone?"

"There is you and me, enough for the present."

"You are one of the Ellri."

"Yes."

"Why can't you fix everything?"

"We have."

"But Blodcroew is going to win."

"Win?"

"The fight for the island."

"He will have won nothing. Blodcroew thinks that he will rule the island from his High Seat at Vangorfold, but the battle is not for Shelter Island, nor for Husgard. The battle, Brador Halar, is for the Fragile Lands, for Birdfolc and Earth-dweller, for the restoration of Fridorfold. If Blodcroew rules, he must rule what remains of the Earth."

"How?"

"The giant snake secretly held captive in the dungeons of Vangorfold Stronghold is Wyrm, a beast born of Blodcroew's sorcery. Blodcroew brought Wyrm to the Fragile Lands to poison its rivers and streams with the serpent's offspring. He means to kill every Earth-dweller and take possession of the Fragile Lands."

"You have to stop him," said Cary, thinking now of his parents, his grandmother and his friends.

"We have."

A whirlwind suddenly blew up a swirling cloud of sand. Cary instinctively covered himself with his wings.

"Remember the Song."

When Cary unwrapped his wings, he was standing alone on a sandy beach, but it was not the same. The grains of sand were coarser, the colours subdued, the sea air a little heavier. He had returned to Shelter Island.

Cary wondered if the white beach and Adarel had been a dream. But it was not a dream. He had not returned from the Realm of Ellri empty-handed. Around his waist was a finely woven belt fitted with a scabbard fringed with gold. Above the scabbard protruded the grip of a sword. On the end of the grip was a round, engraved pommel.

Cary took hold of the grip and slid out the sword. Its blade was long and light and polished so brightly that it mirrored a contorted image of his face. Facing the sea, Cary whispered two broad passes of the sword. His third stroke spun him around.

A wing beat away, their golden mail glinting in the

sun, each with a wing held down and to the side in threat, their pinioned swords laid bare, were three Gildenhyrn.

When the sword Cary wielded flashed before the trio of warriors, their threatening postures wavered. The Gildenhyrn could pick out a sword of Ellri from a thousand, even if it were smeared with mud. Cary's shone as if had been finished and polished an hour before.

The puzzled Husgard warriors darted beaks to one another. Cary sprang at the chance. He did what he had often done. He flew, but this time with skill and power, enough to challenge the best of the Gildenhyrn. The three Gildenhyrn swept up behind him in a moment, immediately joined by two others from the Watcher's Wood.

Cary flew straight over the Watcher's Wood, now closely guarded by the Gildenhyrn. He flew for the Golden Fields, for the mountains. Caught by surprise, the Gildenhyrn had immediately fallen behind but were closing the gap.

Cary had climbed over the Golden Fields, the open chase drawing the attention of the hundreds of Gildenhyrn in the trees of the Watcher's Wood and the many archers posted along the border of Arafen. Every Husgard warrior was on alert, including Clarisse, who was as surprised as any bird on Shelter Island at what was unfolding.

The pursuit quickly became a test of endurance, giving the advantage to Cary with his larger, stronger wings. He flew higher, trying to find a tailwind to increase his speed.

When Cary angled to a steep ascent, the Gildenhyrn were forced to break formation. At a thousand feet, he found the tailwind he needed to outpace the warriors, but the trouble behind had chased him into trouble ahead.

Vultori, who controlled and patrolled the Muna Mountains west of the Golden Fields, were circling the skies, tiny dots on the horizon, six, as Cary counted. He placed both arms back along his side. The grip of his sword was locked in his right hand, the blade lying back along his leg as an extension of his arm. Cary flew straight ahead, every strong sweep of his wings pushing him ahead of the tail-wind. He was flying faster than his wings had ever carried him.

On the approach of an unknown threat from enemy territory, the Vultori formed a staggered formation, one Vultor banking away, presumably to alert the fighting Dreygar.

Gold mail flashed on one side, black wings smudged the sky on the other, all converging on Cary, the lone dark figure in the middle.

The Vultori weilded long blades, but the hulking birds were slow. Cary hatched a plan. He had no wish to battle the Vultori but to break their line and head straight for the Lost Veil. He targeted the lead Vultor at the head of the V-formation, the largest.

At fifty body-lengths and closing, Cary gauged the air passing over his wings as he prepared for a tight barrel roll. At ten lengths, he gripped his sword. At five body lengths, he pulled in his wings and rolled, dropping him slightly beneath the charging Vultor. Mid-roll, on his back, he stalled and swept his sword up from his side. The clash between sword and wing almost knocked the sword from Cary's hand, but the bright sword had accomplished its work. He completed his roll and flew straight through the empty space of the v-formation without another encounter.

Cary momentarily pulled up. A wounded black Vultor,

its large wing disabled, was spiralling down to the western reaches of the Golden Fields. Cary resumed his flight.

In a few minutes, he would gain the mountains. The Gildenhyrn met the Vultori squad in a clash of metal and talon. Gildenhyrn warriors were a third the Vultoris' size but were more agile and better sword wielders. Two more Vultori tumbled from the sky at the first pass, but there would not be a second. One of the Gildenhyrn sounded an alarm. Dreygar, in numbers too high to count, had launched from the lower Vulton Crags.

The Gildenhyrn were vastly outnumbered, so the squad retreated for the refuge of the Watcher's Wood. The golden-armoured birds flew down to the Golden Fields for camouflage. In range of the Watcher's Wood, the retreating warriors summoned help. The Watcher's Wood erupted. A thousand Gildenhyrn launched to the aid of the five.

Cary had led the warriors of Husgard into their first battle.

CHAPTER TWENTY-TWO

Back Again

Watching the battle over the Golden Fields from below, the crowded sky seemed a galaxy of small planes performing acrobatic marvels in a crazy air show. But on closer inspection, it was aerial combat at its most perilous. No two squadrons of birds, on earth or over Shelter Island, were more skilled at aerial combat than the Gildenhyrn and the Dreygar. The warriors were equally matched in skill, but that was where their similarities ended. The Gildenhyrn were renowned for bravery and honour, the Dreygar infamous for treachery.

Like Cary, these warriors of the sky had weapons, light, pinioned swords hidden among the primary feathers of each wing, swords not used clumsily. Flight and fight made deadly encounters appear graceful. Two birds passed in close quarters, one in a roll, the other with its wings extended below itself tip to tip. In the next instant, one of those birds tumbled wounded out of the sky.

If it were not for the support of the archers below, the battle would have brought heavy losses to both sides. Clarisse had helped lead the archers' attack. Pairs of archers had flown low into range of the Dreygar, one archer flying guard while the other took careful aim at her target. Flanked unawares, the Dreygar retreated. The Gildenhyrn had held the hour, thanks to the archers' support.

Husgard had won the day, but the clash brought ill news. Vangorfold's numbers had grown. Squadrons and leaders were better trained. Clearly, Blodcroew and Harfan had been preparing the Dreygar and Vultori for some time. A terrible force would soon be unleashed on Husgard.

Mandwar was also told of the Gildenhyrns' encounter with Cary on the beach below the Watcher's Wood before the boy's westward flight. This bewildering news would have added to the distress were it not for the Gildenhyrn's report of the sword. There was no doubt. Cary wielded a sword of Ellri.

"Somehow, somewhere," Mandwar wondered aloud, "Brador Halar has visited the Realm of Ellri and has been given a task."

"You should stop thinking aloud," said Dearth from behind the owl. "You give away secrets! Isn't that true, Clarisse?"

"I have heard a few..." Clarisse began.

"True! Just as I said," interrupted Dearth.

"This is one secret I am glad of you hearing," said the owl. "Brador Halar has met a Singer of Ellri, for no folc can lay a feather or finger on a sword of Ellri unless the extraordinary weapon is offered. I only wish the boy had come to us. Three Gildenhyrn flushed him like a grouse and chased him to the mountains. Where he is going, and why, I cannot guess."

"If you had asked me that question some time ago," offered Dearth, "I would have said he was flying for home, but now, with a sword of Ellri? He has fled Vangorfold for a reason. Harfan, as we know, is with the Dreygar on the Vulton Crags, so Cary cannot be seeking the old crow. Wyrm has likely slithered into some deep pit. Its foul offspring is poisoning the Fragile Lands with their slime. As far as that snake charmer Blodcroew is concerned, not a creature has seen wing or wattle of him."

"For that we can thank Aevi," added Mandwar. "He has seen him on the High Seat at Vangorfold Stronghold.

"He has gone to kill the snake," said Clarisse, too low for Dearth and Mandwar to hear.

"You have spoken Ascentor Arithi?" asked Mandwar.

Clarisse stood straighter and spoke louder, bearing herself like a true warrior of the Gildenhyrn. "Cary is flying to the Fragile Lands to kill Wyrm, and I have to help him."

Dearth and Madward paused.

Ever irritated by indecision and never shy of danger, Dearth broke the silence. "I shall, if Arithi permits, accompany the Ascentor!"

Mandwar was certain if he had to choose two to carry the battle to the Fragile Lands, it would be Dearth and Arithi.

"You shall, but not without escort."

Mandwar summoned Ofost and Gren. Clarisse, Dearth, Ofost and Gren would head north over the Far Fen to the Muna Mountains. The Dreygar would be too busy tending to their wounded to be vigilantly watching so far north.

Ofost and Gren would have to watch for Vultori spies, but so far north, the threat would be minimal. With Dearth slung below Ofost and Gren and Clarisse flying above, the four flew for the Fragile Lands.

Long before the leaders of Husgard rallied to help Cary, he had flown past the Muna Mountains and over the Western Waste, pursued by three Dreygar. It had been a race for the Lost Veil.

When he flew into the first billowing grey mists of the Lost Veil, he rushed forward, heedless of the Dreygar at his heels. Cary did not know how much the Dreygar feared the Veil's power and that the fierce fighting birds would not enter it, so he flew blindly on, weaving this way and that, not for a moment fearing he would be swallowed up in the Veil's disorienting fog.

Cary finally slowed. He had not been followed. But after three more strokes of his wings a powerful updraft carried him straight up, as if he were a feather in a billowing chimney. Just as suddenly, he plummeted into an airless chasm as if his wings were were cast in iron. When he recovered, he flew on in fog so sluggish, it reminded him of the stagnant Soltin Myrr. Distant voices calling him by name, floated into the eerie silence. Cary swung his sword in the direction of each beckoning invitation, expecting some foul creature to emerge from the fog.

Wherever he pointed the sword, the mists withdrew, so he held the long, shining blade in front of him. He flew on, sword pointed ahead, the heavy fog rushing away from the tip of his sword like frightened wispy ghosts.

The haunting calls faded one by one until a single voice remained, faint at first, as if from a distance. It was Adarel's song, but not his voice. The singing drifted in and out of the grey mists, getting closer and moving farther away, compelling Cary to point his sword in the direction of the singing.

He was back.

CHAPTER TWENTY-THREE
The Final Breath

Striking through the last foggy grip of the Veil, Cary flew directly to the land below. The singing had led him to the very meadow where Gregory had seen Blodcroew and his conjured serpent, Wyrm.

Cary had no need to draw his sword, his weapon of the Ellri held tirelessly in hand since wounding the Vultor. So familiar its grip, so supple its blade, he wielded the sword like an extension of his own arm. His sword faithfully leading, he found the smooth trail Dearth had found days before. The winding trail led him to an outcrop of rocks and the mouth of the serpent's cave.

Cary found eggs strewn over the floor of the dimly lit vault. Many shells now lay empty and dry, others freshly broken, their slimy membranes wet underfoot. But the bulk of the clutch had not hatched.

Sure that the giant Wyrm was not inside the cave, Cary did not hesitate. He thrust his sword into the first unhatched egg. The slimy membrane on his blade sizzled and beaded like water drops jumping across a searing, hot frying pan. The egg burst open and began to wither. It shrank into a pale, wrinkled slug in a bubbling, slimy puddle. Moments later, the bubbling mass hardened, cracks spreading through it that sounded like shuffling feet on thin ice. Then the cracked lump crumbled into a mound of thick, chalky dust.

Encouraged, Cary pierced another egg, then another. He struck every hollow shell, cut through every membrane fresh or old. The sword turned it all to dust. Cary stopped to count. Only three pale eggs remained. He raised his sword to finish the gruesome task.

A hiss curled into his ear.

He turned, swinging his sword at the same time. The blade cut the air. Had it been Wyrm, Cary would have been immediately struck, but the writhing serpent, coiling out of the shadows behind him, was a hatchling barely a week out of its shell.

Out of range of his sword, its head raised to Cary's height, the serpent arched back for a strike. It lunged. Cary tripped back on his heels and fell back on his wings to the dirt floor. The lithe serpent wasted no time. It coiled to Cary's feet and raised its head, its mouth wide, its needle-like fangs barred, and exhaled a hiss before its final deadly strike.

Struggling off his back, Cary levelled the sword at the serpent's weaving head. It hesitated and coiled back. Cary stood up and spread his wings. The startled snake threw itself at his left wing. Cary retracted his wing, twisted to avoid the strike, and slashed down with his sword. The snake never recoiled. Its head lay on the dirt floor, sizzling, its long body withering where it fell.

Cary slashed the three remaining eggs. Satisfied he had not missed a fragment of shell, or a ribbon of slime, he left the dully lit stone vault, its floor covered with mounds of pale ash. The stench was gone. The poisonous spell was broken. But Wyrm remained.

"Kill Wyrm," deduced Cary, "and the rest of its offspring will die with the conjured serpent."

Standing at the mouth of Wyrm's lair, Cary ran his thumb along the fuller of his sword. How would he ever defeat Wyrm? He had barely survived a fight with one of the serpent's hatchlings.

And what of Blodcroew? The disgraced leader had changed. Through the song, the Singers of Ellri had turned the striking black raven white as a spectral corpse, and the blood welling up in Blodcroew's eyes had marked the raven forever with the misery he had brought on so many. No sorcery could remove the stain.

But the blood-red tears and his ghostly coat only enraged Blodcroew and deepened his resolve.

Seeing the raven in his new form erased all doubt among the Birdfolc of Vangorfold that the ancient outcast had returned from a times past. They had respected the black raven; now, the white ghost with the blood-red tears stoked their hearts with dread. Blodcroew had Vangorfold in his grip.

It did not take long before Blodcroew discovered Cary had deserted his throne and had, by all reports, flown for home, but the white raven did not pursue him; the damage had been done. The ghostly raven would have preferred

Cary fight his own siblings; keeping them pitted against each other would defeat the Song, but Blodcroew was content. The cowardly Ascentor had deserted his brother and sister and fled the battle.

Blodcroew had waited and plotted for many turns of the earth. It was time for the final act. The ancient white raven would attack Husgard Hellir to distract its leaders from the world of Bottom-feeders. Husgard would fall; the Fragile Lands would follow.

Blodcroew planned to attack the stronghold of Husgard on the ground and in the sky. He expected Mandwar would retreat to the caves to protect his folc, turning their stronghold into a prison long enough for Blodcroew to establish his reign over the island.

As Blodcroew had predicted, Mandwar had ordered all those under his protection into the caverns of Husgard. He had placed Aevi under the wing of three valiant Gildenhyrn. The plan for the young Ascentor's escape and flight home to the Fragile Lands was in place. It was left now to defend the golden caves of Husgard, the last hope of Fridorfold.

On the plateau above Soltin Myrr, the Dreygar and Vultori had been receiving reports, from various sources, that Raven Wing had undergone a transformation hardly to be believed. Blodcroew was the name on the tongue of every Dreygar and Vultor when the white raven was spotted flying over Soltin Myrr toward the Crags.

When Blodcroew landed in their midst, the Dreygar and Vultori shrank back in fear, forming a wide circle around the ancient ghost. If Blodcroew was an enemy, they were doomed; if an ally and leader, the day of battle would be theirs.

The old crow, Harfan, had not retreated with the others but stood apart, waiting to greet Blodcroew. Harfan had been secretly meeting the raven and had joined in the final plot to destroy Husgard.

The white raven held his wings extended to each side, displaying each distinct point of every primary feather and a long, piniorned sword on each wing. Exultant, as if celebrating freedom from a long imprisonment, Blodcroew held his wings spread in a display of aggression and power.

"The end of Husgard, the beginning of the new world and our reign begins. Prepare for victory."

In a ghastly show of power, the Vultori raised their expansive black wings, brandishing dark swords. The Dreygar, quick and decisive, followed suit.

"This night," Blodcroew continued, "the straw of the Yellow Fields will be strewn with golden mail! You know your errand: the fall of Husgard!"

Blodcroew paused for a moment, drawing the expectant eyes of the fiercest. He lowered his voice. "Bring me the boy—alive, and fly at my right wing."

Blodcroew lifted his voice again. "Death or dishonour! Fly!" The white raven let out a piercing shriek that some Dreygar swore afterward split the rock of the Vulton Crags.

The western sky filled with the dark storm, but Blodcroew was not at the head. The white raven flew low over Soltin Myrr before he passed over the forests in Vangorfold territory along the Vangorian Pass. Chosen Dreygar joined him as he flew seaward. Far out to sea, Blodcroew would turn north before heading back to the island. Unexpected, when the storm was raging over the Golden

Fields, he would fall on Husgard's gates from the sea.

The archers posted along Arafen and the Freewind were the first to raise the alarm. A black storm had risen from the Vulton Crags. Messengers relayed a report to the Gildenhyrn in the Watcher's Wood. Foxes were dispatched with messages for the Gildenhyrn hiding in the Golden Fields, archers by their sides waiting to let their arrows fly into the approaching black mass of wings. Arrows spent, the archers would head for the cover of Arafen.

The main force of Gildenhyrn, relying on their luminous sky-coloured undersides for camouflage, would descend on the writhing black sea from above. It was left to a brave contingent of Gildenhyrn, waiting for Mandwar's signal in the Watcher's Wood, to meet the storm head-on.

Mandwar hoped the unsuspecting enemy would believe the main force of Gildenhyrn were making a head-on assault. From below, Gildenhyrn and archers would further distract the attackers while the main force of Gildenhyrn would strike from above. Though outnumbered, Mandwar hoped the tactic would send the enemy into confusion and turn the concerted attack into a panicked retreat.

All of Husgard was waiting for the lone white figure of Mandwar to fly low over the eastern edge of the Golden Fields to signal the assault. Mandwar was waiting atop the highest tree, where Arafen, the Freewind and the Watcher's Wood converged.

All eyes were to the darkening west. It was the final breath.

CHAPTER TWENTY-FOUR

The Battle For Husgard

Mandwar had seen the coming storm before many of the archers who were posted further west along the edge of Arafen. For the Gildenhyrn and archers awaiting the owl's signal flight, wind and river, sun and earth had paused for one last breath. At the chosen moment, just as the hush became unbearable, like a white firegast against a black storm, Mandwar unfurled his great wings and in one sweep lifted from his perch.

Hundreds of Gildenhyrn launched into flight as if startled by a single shot. In a few moments, flight formations were patterned across the evening sky, staggered V's, single lines and columns all coordinated with a special task to divide the more haphazard onslaught of Vultori and the treacherous Dreygar.

When every eye of the advancing dark army was fixed on the Gildenhyrn rushing to engage head-on, the Husgard archers rose from their hiding places in the Golden Fields, loosing every arrow from their quivers into the black cloud. Birds fell like black rain. Every arrow spent, the archers flew straight for the protection of Arafen to replenish quivers and take positions high in the trees.

Among the archers, the fiercest of the Gildenhyrn shot up like rockets from the field below and pierced the dark cloud in barrel rolls, pinioned swords striking with every revolution.

The first phase of the assault divided the massive dark cloud in half; half for the Gildenhyrn springing from the Watcher's Wood, who were now driving enemy targets into range of the re-armed archers in the trees of Arafen, the other half reserved for the Gildenhyrn who had shot up through the dark cloud and dived back down.

It was left to the remaining Gildenhyrn, camouflaged high above the battle, to deliver the decisive blow. The golden warriors fell on the divided sides of Blodcroew's army like hail, striking confused Vultori and Dreygar flying in every direction.

Mandwar's strategy had worked, but even in the confusion created by Husgard's three-fold attack, the fierce enemy fighters, driven by an unknown fear, threw themselves into battle, desperately attempting to overwhelm the Gildenhyrn and Husgard by sheer numbers like leaves smothering a fire.

Instead of retreating, the storm had only spread across the sky. Mandwar returned to Husgard to signal Aevi's escape. On his flight he received report of an assault from the sea. Outnumbered, the troop of Gildenhyrn guarding Husgard were struggling to defend the cavern's mouth.

The frontal assault over the Golden Fields had been a

diversion for the white raven's direct attack on Husgard. Mandwar veered low in another direction to avoid the main entrance. He flew instead for a secret entrance into Husgard, closer to the sea.

It had escaped even the attentive mind of Mandwar that in the end Aevi would hold the key to the final outcome of the battle. When the three Gildenhyrn charged with guarding Aevi had first got wind of the direct attack on Husgard, they took the boy deeper into the caves to the Dome of Times Passing. The chamber was closest to the secret passage that led out of Husgard's high cliffs, where they would, if necessary, make their planned escape. Two Gildenhyrn stood guard outside the chamber's entrance and one within. Gregory, as he had so many times with Mandwar, was looking up into the woven threads of gold from the moment he arrived.

The spaces between the branches of gold had turned deep blue, like the evening sky. But on this occasion it was different. No images appeared. But the sky and the stars beyond seemed more real, as if he could pass through the branches into the sky beyond. And the branches were moving and twisting as if Gregory were watching roots grow in a time-lapse film.

But they weren't growing. The branches extended and retracted, over and over again. It was as if the branches were trying to break free of the stone ceiling.

While he watched, hand in his pocket, Gregory had been fingering the little objects he had collected at Husgard. "Hmm? What's that?", He pulled out the small golden feather that he had pocketed when the Gildenhyrn first soared out of the swirling fog at home.

Gregory walked to the middle of the chamber under

the dome of branches, holding the feather in front of him to compare it with those on the pedestal. The feather was the same shape of the feathers that decorated the stone. Every feather was the same as the one cradled in his hand, finely carved as a relief against the stone.

On his tippy toes, Gregory ran his fingers over the flat top of the short column. A singular feather, not as a relief, but its opposite, like a tiny decorative stamp, was carved into the stone. Instinctively, Gregory pressed his feather into the mould. It fit...

The moment Gregory fitted the feather to the mould, every feather on the pedestal suddenly brightened. The golden branches of the dome that Gregory had seen lengthening and shrinking back sprang to life, twisting, curling and lengthening. The Gildenhyrn guarding Gregory became alarmed and went to inform the others. One of the two warriors posted outside the chamber returned.

"The dome is getting bigger," he said, the curling golden branches growing wilder by the second.

Piercing screeches and a clash of steel rang up the passageway. Dreygar had found an escape passage and had fought their way into the caves. Gregory and his two guardians were trapped.

The growing golden branches threaded across the entrance to the chamber and tangled into a thick web. The two Gildenhyrn watched the branches weave a tight impenetrable door, leaving small gaps fit only for a mouse.

"Look," said Gregory, pointing straight up to the dome. His two protectors raised their hooked beaks. The branches had greatly increased the height and circumference of the dome, as if the golden braided branches had pushed up the ceiling, creating much larger spaces between the branches. Gregory flew up between the forks of a large branch.

"The sky!" Gregory shouted below into the golden chamber. Without hesitating, his two guardians flew up. With Gregory between them, Gregory's guards escaped Husgard and headed north over the Far Fells. Once out of danger, his guardians would steer Gregory west toward the Wild Waste, the Lost Veil and the Fragile Lands beyond.

The battle over the Golden Fields had turned. The sheer numbers of Vultori and Dreygar were overwhelming the strategies and skill of the Gildenhyrn, pushing the defenders back toward the caves of Husgard and the Watcher's Wood.

Mandwar, meanwhile, had entered the passageways of Husgard to find its branches of gold growing and curling through the surrounding rock as if the caves had been carved in sand. Cracking stone and the alarmed shouts of those within the stronghold were all he could hear.

When Mandwar got word that Aevi had escaped to the Lost Veil, he ordered the evacuation of Husgard north to the Far Fells, a barren landscape offering very little cover against enemies. But there was little else.

Mandwar flew to the tip of the tallest pine. From this vantage point, even at a great distance, a heartbeat would throb into his ear. He watched as the hundreds of Birdfolc erupted from the security of the Husgard caves, fleeing over the cliffs for the Far Fells. The Gildenhyrn would protect their folc to the last warrior. This would be the last flight and fight for Husgard and the hope of Fridorfold.

Mandwar's attention to the escape was broken by a loud shriek of command. Over the treetops of Arafen he found its source. Atop the tallest pine in the forest, pale white against the dark clouds behind, perched the figure of Blodcroew.

Mandwar unfurled his wings and launched into a low glide through the treetops.

CHAPTER TWENTY-FIVE

Clarisse's Bow

Led by Dearth's infallible nose, Clarisse, Gren and Ofost quickly found the serpent's den and discovered the small mounds of ash, all that remained of the slain offspring of Wyrm. Gren and Ofost flew over the area in search of Cary.

"He's been here," Clarisse said.

"And left," added Dearth, "through here."

Dearth, having preserved his nimble Fridorfold stature roughly half a human's height, with Clarisse close behind, cut a straight path over the side-winding furrows left by Wyrm, following Cary's footprints. The two scouts stepped out into sunlight. The sun was streaking through tall pines, spilling steeply down into a bright meadow completely encircled by trees.

Beyond the far side of the meadow, Ofost and Gren were hovering over the trees. The excited pair had found something. Dearth bounded and Clarisse slid and stumbled down the steep hill. The agile rat leapt across the meadow with such speed that Clarisse was left standing on the opposite side.

"Cary has found Wyrm," Dearth shouted back.

When Clarisse finally reached the trees on the other side of the meadow, Dearth had sprung off in the direction of Gren and Ofost, who were now diving back and forth at the level of the treetops. As Clarisse ran forward from tree to tree, a great crashing of branches and splashing of water echoed through the wood.

When she reached a tree that gave her a partial view of the river, she stopped to catch her breath. In truth, she was afraid, and with each breath, the young Ascentor was expelling her fear and shoring up her courage. She slid an arrow from her quiver and nocked it on the bowstring. With another breath, she slid around the large tree and started down a path that would lead her straight to the river battle, but she was too late.

Dearth had found Cary on the shore of the river braced for an attack, his sword pointed up at the serpent. The fearless rat scampered up the snake's curving spine and struck with both his long knives just above its wings. The tips of Dearth's long knives barely penetrated the shielding scales. But it was enough. Wyrm thrashed and twisted violently with the needling pain, throwing Dearth into the river. Dearth pulled himself free from the strong current, as sopped as a drowned rat.

Gren and Ofost swooped down low from behind, threatening the serpent with brandished swords. With the threat of a long shining sword in front and two behind, Wyrm flew straight up. Gren was hit with a sweep of one of the serpent's large sinewy wings and spiralled to the riverbank.

Dearth was stranded on the wrong side of the river. Gren had barely avoided a plunge himself. Ofost did not know whom to help first. Deciding she could not carry Dearth safely on her own, she flew to Gren. Cary, meanwhile, had flown up from the river's edge and was pursuing the serpent just above the treetops back toward the meadow.

Clarisse ran with her armed bow back to the edge of the meadow. Not wasting a moment, she loosed an arrow. Unaware of Clarisse's presence, the serpent knocked it aside with a flap of its bat-like wing. She launched another. This one got the serpent's attention. It lodged just behind its jaw. Wyrm twisted, its slit eyes cast like daggers to the stab of pain. Cary followed the same sight line of the serpent. Bow in hand, Clarisse had braced for another shot.

But Wyrm abandoned the threat of stinging thorns to first destroy the lethal metal fang. The serpent turned back to Cary and coiled for a strike. Cary was ready. Bracing itself with a strong down-sweep of its grisly wings, the serpent lunged at Cary. In a single burst of his wings, Cary propelled up. Legs bent, two feet on the back of the serpent's head, Cary launched to safety. Wyrm had attacked the same way its offspring had. The serpent retracted and flapped forward for another strike.

Spurred on by her brother's narrow escape, her bow and arrow poised, Clarisse flew up and hovered, as best as she was able, a bowshot behind the serpent. She dare not fire at the serpent now for fear of missing and hitting Cary on the opposite side, so she flew a little to the side to keep Cary out of her line of fire and her out of sight of Wyrm's darting black-slit eye.

Clarisse pulled back her bowstring. She would fire two

arrows in quick succession, the first to turn the serpent's head, the second, through its mouth into its throat. She flew closer.

Just before she released her fingers from the bowstring, Clarisse had a strange impulse to sing, the words and melody welling up in her mind and heart like a battle song. She had often joined in the old songs of the Birdfolc, but at Husgard, not over a field of battle. It was strange to have the urge to sing in the face of such chaos. She slackened her bow. She could not hold the song back: "In times of old, Of battles told, When arrows loosed, From archers bold, Strike your foe For Fridorfold."

One short stanza was all it took. Wyrm's head stopped weaving as if struck motionless by a spell. It reeled around, hissing, searching for the source of what had wounded its dark mind.

It flashed its long, forked tongue to smell the air. What was this new foe that wielded a power in the old tongue? Before Wyrm instinctively whipped out its tongue again, Clarisse loosed an arrow. The bolt hit its mark.

The great flying serpent flailed its head, trying to dislodge the arrow that had passed halfway through its tongue. Cary did not waste the advantage. He flew under the serpent. Cary below, Gren instinctively flew in front of the serpent to distract it.

Wyrm suddenly broke the arrow, but not without tearing its tongue. The enraged serpent turned to fasten its ragged-toothed jaws onto Gren.

The light-coloured underside of Wyrm's throat loomed over Cary. He beat his wings straight up, sword gripped in both hands, arms extended, transformed into a javelin.

Any other sword might have turned on the scales of

the conjured serpent, but this sword was a gift of the Ellri, forged for its purpose. Cary struck his mark. The blade pierced the underside of Wyrm's jaw, as if its scaled skin were thick, wet paper. The sword slid straight in to its full length. Cary had flown with such force, the sword hilt alone stopped the blade from going further.

Stunned, one wing numbed, he reeled off like a wounded bird and spiralled to the ground. Wyrm had gone limp the instant it had been struck, so deadly was Cary's strike. The winged beast lolled and dropped from the sky, filling half the meadow with its toxic, ringed coils. Somewhere below the ruined Wyrm lay Cary.

The prolonged battle, fought over river, forest and meadow, had ended in an instant.

Clarisse, Ofost and Gren flew to the ground. Dearth was the first to find Cary. He had been narrowly missed by a free-falling coil of the snake and lay covered with a bent and lifeless wing of Wyrm. He was stunned, his left arm numb, but with the help of Dearth, the young swordsman found his feet.

"Cary." Clarisse threw one arm over Cary's good shoulder, slipped her other arm under his useless limb and hugged him. She whispered to him. "I knew you would come back."

Dazed, Cary returned the hug with his working arm as best he could. "I've seen Adarel."

Gren and Ofost, Dearth and Clarisse exchanged looks.

"I've been to the Realm of Ellri – I was standing on a beautiful white beach." Cary was trying to shake off his whirling dizziness. "Adarel gave me this sword..." Not yet free of the consequence of flying full-force into Wyrm's gullet and his subsequent tumble to the ground, Cary broke off, pawing at his empty scabbard and searching the ground for his sword.

Dearth broke in, "We will retrieve your sword together, young Brador Halar, Serpent Slayer."

For a moment the oddly dressed, oversized rat stood before Cary a complete stranger. Then, the image of Dearth scampering up the serpent's spine splashed across his memory.

"Did you have a good ride?" asked Cary, the corner of his mouth turned up in the beginning of a smile.

"A rat should not be the one to tame a snake," Dearth answered with a long grin.

Ofost and Gren alighted nearby. Dearth led everyone to Wyrm's upturned head.

Cary continued, "If I were alone, Wyrm would have..."

"Nonsense!" erupted Dearth. "The boy has lost his senses! Wyrm is dead! The sword that killed the beast is sticking out the bottom of its gullet. Whose sword is that, pray tell?"

Dearth pointed to the hilt and pommel of Cary's sword, feigned a search for his own swords, which he had already retrieved. "It is certainly not one of mine."

Gren and Ofost stood back while Cary, Clarisse and Dearth walked to the underside of Wyrm's head. On its side, Wyrm's head stood taller than Dearth, its scaled skin silvery grey though rapidly fading.

Cary lightly took hold of the pommel and slipped his hand down the grip. With his one good arm, his foot braced against Wyrm, he hauled out the blade. The sorcery broken, Wyrm turned stiff and white as bone. It held its sculptured pose only for a moment before the fossilized Wyrm cracked, crumbled; then collapsed into a mound of powder as fine as if it had been ground by a mortar and pestle.

Cary wiped the blade on the grass and lifted the sword. The beautiful object had escaped his scrutiny until then, so occupied had his mind and heart been. It was longer than he remembered, straight and sure, polished, with intricate designs on either side.

The weapon was a sword of Ellri. Of that Dearth had no doubt. He was as interested as Cary in examining it. Cary handed the sword to Dearth.

"It has inscribed your story on the blade," said Dearth.

Cary sidled up to Dearth. Along each flat side of the fuller, miniature etched scenes, beginning with his first flight with the Gildenhyrn, decorated the blade. There was a picture of his arrival at the stronghold of Vangorfold, an image of him at his place on the High Seat and another of his flight over the Golden Fields, each one inlaid into the metal in silver filigree. Whether before or after, the sword had also inscribed an image of the battle with Wyrm.

Curious, Clarisse passed her bow through her hands. She found similarly inscribed tableaux growing in both directions from the grip, like a flowering vine. Like Cary's sword, scenes of Clarisse's adventure were illustrated like the old illuminated manuscripts belonging to her parents, but with one difference: the craftwork did not stop with the ruin of Wyrm. Like an arrow that had been shot beyond its target, the pictures continued into the future.

Clarisse could not understand what she was seeing. Ofost came to her side.

"Gren," Ofost said solemnly, "we shall never again fly over the Golden Fields."

CHAPTER TWENTY-SIX
Fly or Fall

Silent, graceful as he was deadly, like a white firegast against the backdrop of the darkened forest below and the gathering dark grey clouds to the West, Mandwar glided toward his enemy.

He approached unheeded.

Blodcroew was taller than the owl remembered and, as accurately as he could guess, larger than himself. But this did not discourage Mandwar. In the owl's experience, the smaller, more courageous bird could easily gain the advantage in fight and flight; Blodcroew was but a larger target.

The white raven was watching the battle that had now moved over the Watcher's Wood. Mandwar slid toward his target on silent wings.

The ghastly blood-red tears that marked Blodcroew in punishment for the misery he had brought on the ancient Birdfolc of Fridorfold steeled Mandwar's courage. The Guardian of Husgard let out a piercing cry, calling Blodcroew to battle.

Blodcroew turned his head as casually as he would at council. But he did not launch to meet the challenge. As if Blodcroew had been shot from his perch, the large, ghostly raven dropped headlong into the trees.

Mandwar circled back and returned to where he had seen Blodcroew plunge through the tree tops. He swept down among a few tall pines and alighted on a low branch. He surveyed the forest floor. Curiously, Blodcroew was standing on the ground a short glide away, his back to Mandwar.

"Stinga Backstabber," Blodcroew grated, not turning to address Mandwar, "do you think I cracked the shell a short turn ago, or have you simply grown short-sighted? You should have brought your squeaking yellow nursemaids."

In that same moment a chorus of heartbeats drummed from the surrounding branches of nearby trees. Blodcroew had laid a trap. Dreygar were in the trees. An arrow was nocked. An archer's bow flexed and creaked. Three Dreygar emerged from the trees beyond Blodcroew.

Undeterred, Mandwar attacked.

In a sudden flash of wings, the three Dreygar hopped over Blodcroew to intercept Mandwar. With a single stroke of his long, pinioned swords, Mandwar slashed the wings of the Dreygar at each end of the trio in unison. The wounded fighters dropped to the ground. Talons outstretched, Mandwar clutched and twisted both wings of the third Dreygar in the middle. Arrows flew and missed, one passing through the splayed feathers of Mandwar's outstretched wing. Blodcroew fled through the trees. Mandwar gave chase. A troop of shrieking Dreygar followed.

Gildenhyrn had flown to help Mandwar after several had spotted the owl over Arafen. The moment Mandwar's rescuers arrived, Blodcroew erupted out of the trees, followed closely by Mandwar. The Dreygar were in close pursuit. The Gildenhyrn and Dreygar collided in a flurry of feather and sword, leaving Mandwar in lone pursuit of Blodcroew.

Effortlessly, Blodcroew led Mandwar high above the Golden Fields. The white raven was flying in the direction of circling Vultori. Three or four Gildenhyrn, including Vaskar, withdrew from the skirmish when the Dreygar deserted the fight.

As Blodcroew and Mandwar approached the distant Vultori, the landscape below stole Mandwar's attention. The golden threads that had long illuminated the passageways of Husgard, that had brought comfort to all living under their glow, had grown into giant golden curling tendrils that were entangling and felling trees, twisting and coiling up the Freewind, swallowing the water like diving golden serpents. Shoots of golden vines were erupting out of the Golden Fields like furious tentacles. Shelter Island was perishing at the very threads of life that had been the light and joy of Husgard. Blodcroew too had seen it, and reeled and screeched as if he had flown into a nightmare.

From out of the chaos, a soft rythmic pulse struck Mandwar deeper than an arrow. It was a heartbeat inscribed on his own, young Aevi. Gregory had been captured. The boy's form hung in the air a short distance ahead, slung in the gruesome claws of the largest of the Vultori.

Mandwar cocked his head back and shouted orders to the Gildenhyrn who had closed the space behind their owl leader. He changed course and flew not at Blodcroew, who was croaking and screeching like an infuriated gryphon, but targeting the great black Vultor.

Two Vultori tried to intercept. Mandwar deftly manoeuvred past. Talons out and ahead, Mandwar struck. The Vultor dropped Gregory. A few beats below, Vaskar and another Gildenhyrn snatched up Aevi by his wings.

Mandwar, his talons locked deep in the giant Vultor below him, was spiralling down toward the Golden Fields, down to the beautiful sea of long grass now intermingled with writhing golden vines.

Mandwar cried out to his heart-struck Gildenhyrn, "Fly! Fly to the Fragile Lands! Husgard ... the island is lost! Fly for your lives! Fly for Fridorfold!"

Blodcroew swept down in pursuit of Mandwar, who was doing his best to dislodge his talons, which were snagged in the tethers of the Vultor's armour. The owl's strong sweeps of his wings managed to keep both him and the lifeless Vultor from falling like stones. On Mandwar's down-stroke, Blodcroew struck.

Blodcroew had merely swept by Mandwar, the tips of his long white wings whispering over Mandwar's back. But the sharp tips of Blodcroew's swords had clipped Mandwar's shoulders.

Mandwar finally released his talons from the great black Vultor beneath him. His beautiful long but maimed wings stretched out above him. Mandwar, Guardian of Husgard and friend of Aevi, fell to the Golden Fields like the largest winged and most beautiful of angels.

It was told later by Vaskar that the vines, curling up and through the Golden Fields, caught the fallen owl, lifted and cradled him, gently passing him from vine to golden vine out to the Mirror Sea.

Vaskar did not follow, but obeyed his commander. The captain and the Gildenhyrn now under his command assailed Blodcroew and his Vultor wing guards with abandon, forcing the overwhelmed warriors to flee in every direction of the compass. Before Blodcroew and his crew could regroup, valiant Gildenhyrn had escaped with Aevi.

As the myriad golden curling branches were devouring Shelter Island, Vaskar ordered an evacuation. He found Aevi and his escorts, then, as did every other creature, he fled for the Fragile Lands.

The Lost Veil was blowing away as if it had only been a morning mist. With Shelter Island lost, the veil removed, the thousands of folc who had called Shelter Island home, abandoned the island as one massive flock. Enemies or friends, Dreygar or Gildenhyrn, young or old, air-lifted in a net or borne on backs, a whole civilization that had been veiled from the people of the Fragile Lands for hundreds of years trained their eyes on their only refuge.

The entire population of Shelter Island began to spread out like an approaching swarm of locusts. The singular swarm separated into scattered haphazard formations, as Birdfolc loyal to Husgard and Vangorfold searched for comrades.

When the cloud of birds reached the continent, united by fear of the Dreygar and wary of Earth-dwellers, most flew for the shelter of Oakenfen, others the seclusion of the mountains or the remote areas of Draugon or the Giant's Finger. Leaderless, the folc of Shelter Island flew and bounded off in every direction of the compass.

The time for Shelter Island had passed, and had begun a new times passing.

CHAPTER TWENTY-SEVEN

The Way Forward

After discussing the scenes etched along the blade of Cary's sword and Clarisse's bow, Dearth was first to lift a nose to the dark swirling cloud, a swarming mass heading for the continent.

"We will go to see this storm falling upon us," said Gren as he and Ofost set off at once.

"It would be better if we found shelter under the trees," Dearth said, suspecting the descending cloud would bring bad news, as well as bad weather.

Clarisse backed up against a tree. "I think we're the right size. At least compared to the trees." Dearth had not changed. He remained stubbornly as tall as Gregory.

Gren and Ofost returned, eyes wide, as if they had seen a ghost.

"Shelter Island has been emptied of every living creature," said Gren, as if his breath had been knocked out of him. "Shelter Island can be our shelter no longer. It has been destroyed—or swallowed up—the Island is gone, just like Clarisse's bow has foretold. We have spoken to other Gildenhyrn—seen other folc—Husgard folc, Vangorfold folc, Dreygar—and Vultori. Friend and foe are fleeing to the continent as one flock. We have seen Blodcroew. He is flying in this direction."

"He must be coming here to tend to his pet," said Dearth.

"Or seeking the cliffs," added Gren.

"What about Gregory?" asked Clarisse, who had been thinking of him for some time. "Did you see him?"

Gren bowed. "No, we did not see Ascentor Aevi."

"Mandwar would not have let anything happen to the young Ascentor," said Dearth.

"Ascentor Arithi," added Gren, "remember Mandwar arranged for Aevi's escape from the island under the care of two of our order. He will be among the folc who have escaped Shelter Island."

"We have to find him—now," said Clarisse, waking up to the responsibilities of her former world. "The Gilden-hyrn will take him home. We need to go home—our parents have probably unhinged, totally." Clarisse was sure her mom would have persuaded the police to conduct a continent-wide search.

It was left to the two Ascentors to decide: stay and meet Blodcroew, who was fast approaching with any number of his former minions, or leave to find Gregory, and regroup.

"Blodcroew will be limited in any widespread damage he can do, at least at present," said Clarisse, sounding a lot like Mandwar. "If any of us should fall, who will continue in the fight for Fridorfold?"

No one could offer an answer to Clarisse's question.

"My sister—Ascentor Arithi—is right," said Cary, catching Clarisse off guard with his whole-hearted approval. "She usually is."

"Our path has been chosen," said Dearth. "We had better keep out of sight or the choice will not be ours."

The Fridorfold leaders quickly ran or flew a safe distance away from Wyrm's ashen remains and hid among a copse of spruce trees with a view to the treetops lining the opposite side of the meadow. The unusual league of friends, bonded by trial and the hope and Song of Fridorfold, watched for the arrival of the white ghost.

In a breath the broad wings of Blodcroew blotted the sky. The white raven spread his wings, stopped himself midair and alighted atop the tallest tree east of the meadow. Like Dearth, he had not diminished in size, but stood almost as tall as Gregory.

The ghost has not lost an ember of his former power, Dearth thought. *And judging by his deathly calm, not a grain of his ancient resolve.*

Blodcroew cocked a large pale eye to the white and grey ash trail that wound a wide path through the meadow, a path unmistakable in form, all that remained of his poisonous designs. It was the ashen scar of his conjured slave, Wyrm.

Unmoved by the wreckage of his sorcery, his years of scheming turned to ash, the white raven cawed, not like a comrade who had lost a friend, not like a leader despairing over years of plans that had blown away like dust, not even in anger, but as a simple command. Two Dreygar and a Vultor alighted in trees near by. Blodcroew offered no acknowledgement.

The island behind the Veil was gone. The battle had

ended not in victory, but with the destruction of the Island, the very territory Blodcroew desired to rule. His throne had been snatched from his talons. Vangorfold was gone. Husgard was gone. But Fridorfold, the hope of Fridorfold had survived.

However, Blodcroew did not dwell on his losses, but exulted. Mandwar and Adarel, the Guardian of Husgard and a Singer of Fridorfold, had been vanquished.

"Folly nests in the foolish heads of those who fell to the Fragile Lands." Blodcroew preened a feather back in its proper place. "The Fridorfold fools are leaderless."

He cocked an eye back to the meadow. "By feather or claw, I will take the Fragile Lands."

After a glance to the sky behind him, the imposing white raven, stained beneath each eye with the blood-red tears of his past deeds, sprang aloft on his pale wings. He flew straight toward the canopy of treetops over the copse of spruce trees where the Fridorfold leaders were hiding. Seconds later, having finally caught up to Blodcroew, a large squad of Dreygar and Vultori followed. In another breath, the sky above the meadow was obliterated by a massive flock of Birdfolc pledged to the white raven, many of whom had been in the last battle over the Golden Fields.

Hidden among the spruce trees, the leaders of Husgard froze, hoping that a quick-eyed Vultor or one of the quick-winged Dreygar would not drop down from the horde to investigate a movement, or a glint of gold from Ofost's or Gren's armour. The last stragglers of the flock passed overhead and Clarisse freed her trapped breath. Gren immediately darted up into the top canopy of trees.

The tireless warrior returned from the treetops moments later. "Blodcroew and his minions will soon be dark spots on the western horizon. We may safely leave if we stay low to the trees."

"Escort our Ascentors home," said Dearth. "And for Fridorfold's sake, keep to remote areas. Stay low. Fly from tree to tree. Walk if you must. The Ascentors must not be seen."

Dearth bounded off into the woods, already intent on what he had to do next. Led by their skilled friends, Cary and Clarisse started the journey home.

EPILOGUE
Just the Beginning

The moment Cary and Clarisse alighted on the back fire escape leading to their apartment, their wings burst into a bright golden flame and vanished. The two would discover later, like the golden threads in the caves of Husgard, their wings were imprinted in golden threads upon their backs, invisible to the eye if seen under electric light but visible at the right angle under a bright sun, or under water, or under the gentle silver beams of the moon. They did not know it, but their wings were merely dormant, waiting for a spark to burst into existence.

Believing their wings gone, Cary and Clarisse had no evidence of their month-long stay on Shelter Island. Gren and Ofost, who could have proven their incredible story, had flown off to join Dearth in his search for Mandwar and had taken Cary's sword and Clarisse's bow for safekeeping. Cary and Clarisse were dressed differently but were not wearing anything that any imaginative brother and sister could not have found around Freeton. When it came time to explain their incredible adventure on Shelter Island, Cary and Clarisse would be on their own.

Standing on the fire escape, they braced themselves for a long and loud lecture. Brother and sister had agreed on the journey home that after two versions of their ridiculous, hare-brained story about talking birds and an island hidden behind a veil were told in detail, even if it were offered by Clarisse, Mom and Dad would send son and daughter for counselling.

They warily lifted the sash of the old window, straddled the ledge and entered the apartment. Clarisse was summoning the imagined faces of two worried parents huddled over maps and police documents and newspaper clippings, when Gregory, wingless, burst out of his bedroom, not a parent in sight. He had been piling, twisting and knotting every pillow, towel or blanket he could reach from the closet.

Gregory charged Cary and hugged his brother harder than he had ever.

"You have to build me a nest-bed," he said. "I want a nest-bed."

Clarisse joined in her brothers' hug. Not one could remember when the three last hugged together. Smothered in the hug, Gregory had not stopped begging Cary to help build his nest-bed. Gregory's rosy cheeked face beamed into Clarisse's teary eyes. She squeezed him safe in her arms.

"The young Ascentor Aevi has spoken," announced Cary, imitating the formal speech of Mandwar, his own tears running down his cheeks. "We shall build you a nest-bed fit for a Fowl King never before seen, even in the golden caves of Husgard!"

Cary and Gregory set to the royally appointed task at

once. Clarisse, curious that no one was home, ventured into the living room and turned on the radio. She returned to Gregory's bedroom a few minutes later, a smile spread across her face. Cary was rolling a blanket into a large tube.

"Cary, you're not going to believe this."

"What?" returned Cary, lifting the rolled blanket onto Gregory's bed.

"Only one day has passed since we left for Shelter Island. It must have been the Lost Veil."

"Or Adarel," added Cary, pushing his brother over the rim of blankets along the edge of his bed.

"Wait'll Mandwar sees this," Gregory said as he wrestled over the rim of his nest-bed to make some final adjustments. A moment later he popped up his head like a chick from its shell.

"I need more pillows."

༄ ABOUT THE AUTHOR ༄

John Paul Tucker holds degrees in Theatre and Theology and has many years experience as an Ontario Certified English Language Teacher, in addition to teaching mime, puppetry and Drama to teens and children. It has furnished him with an eclectic head of ideas.

He is currently celebrating publishing his 50th article on www.thewriterslessonbook.com, an educational website he created for writers, featuring writing tips and techniques harvested from the books we love to read. He has published poems in the Toronto Sun, Little Trinity Print Magazine and Imago Arts e-magazine. His poem City Sidewalks won first prize in a Toronto wide poetry contest. Two of his short stories, The Crooked Tree and The Debt Collector have each won a prize awarded by The Word Guild and The Prescott Journal respectively. You will find one of his fantasy stories recently published in the popular Hot Apple Cider anthology Christmas with Hot Apple Cider. JP has been busy polishing up The Rooster and the Raven King & The Rise of the Crimson King, Books II & III of The Song of Fridorfold trilogy, pursuing Cary, Clarisse and Gregory on their fantastic adventures.

John Paul is excited to be putting the final touches to his fourth novel, a YA fantasy inspired by the remarkable storyteller, George MacDonald. Get the latest news about JP's upcoming novels, watch book trailers, read free stories and poems, send in some art work, take a peek at some photos, or drop by to say hello at his official website www.johnpaultucker.com.

If you have enjoyed reading this book, please consider posting a review on Amazon or Goodreads.

What follows is a **Sample Chapter** of Book Two of the soon-to-be-released Song of Fridorfold trilogy, **THE ROOSTER AND THE RAVEN KING**

CHAPTER ONE

For Fridorfold

"Clarisse, did you see the newspaper this morning?" Cary spread open the paper.

"MASSIVE DARK CLOUD DESCENDS NEAR FREETON—Or look at this one—IS THIS THE NEXT PLAGUE?"

Clarisse stepped into the dining room from the kitchen, balancing a tray laden with plates of sandwiches and three glasses of milk. She stood at the edge of the table, humming, waiting for Cary to catch on.

"Why didn't you say something?" Cary gathered up the newspapers, which he had spread over every inch of the table as if he were about to embark on a complicated craft project.

"Mmm, nice table cloth," Clarisse said. She slid the tray onto the table. "I still can't get my head around the idea," said Clarisse, "we haven't been away—I mean, away from home, for even one entire day. Shelter Island kept its own time."

"I think it was the Veil," added Cary. "When I was flying through it I've never felt more lost in my life."

"Well, it's gone," said Clarisse. "Who's going to believe us if we say we've flown through it anyways? A shape-shifting veil—an island full of talking birds..."

"A rat almost as tall as Gregory," interrupted Cary, "foxes and..."

Clarisse counted her fingers.

"For a month," continued Clarisse, "We were there for at least a month. If we tell Mom and Dad, they'll think we're playing some kind of joke—or we've snapped or something—not to mention our wings."

"Listen to this," Cary spread open a newspaper. "The isolated storm cloud threatening to descend on Freeton vanished into thin air. Witnesses from the immediate area report the cloud was not a weather formation, but a massive flock of large, unidentified birds. Reports yet to be confirmed by authorities."

"Everything seems so complicated now," said Clarisse. "What are we supposed to do?"

"At least the nanny didn't show up," said Cary, folding the paper. "We should probably wait for Dearth. He's usually got a plan."

"Usually?"

Cary and Clarisse started.

"I can see you haven't forgotten your lessons, young Ascentor." Dearth had broken in, helped himself to whatever took his fancy in their pantry and alerted Gregory to his presence, who was standing by his side, without so much as squeezing a creak from the old wooden floors.

"There is news which has not yet found the papers," continued Dearth. "Your parents, it seems, have discovered ancient scrolls, written in a language from a time past, from the days of Fridorfold."

"How do you know they're from Fridorfold?" asked

Cary.

"The material," answered Dearth. "The woven parchment they described is similar to what was used on Shelter Island in a time past, before the island's creation. The scrolls may hold evidence of our shared past with Earth-dwellers, of the past civilization of Fridorfold. If Blodcroew gets his claws on those scrolls, he will destroy them. But that is not the whole of my news—the scrolls have been stolen."

"Stolen?" asked Cary. "How?"

"If I knew the means or the motive, Ascentor Halor, I would be presenting the scrolls to you now," answered Dearth. "The scrolls—six, I think—were placed in three cases, two to a case, and set aside for transport to some facility."

"That would be the F-A-A, the Freeton Antiquities Authority," added Clarisse. "Our parents work there—not all the time, but..."

"Most of the time," interrupted Cary.

"When they're researching, or cataloguing something," Clarisse continued. "They have a laboratory there, at least my mom does—my dad builds models and stuff—it's where they study artifacts. I've been there."

"The scrolls never arrived," said Dearth. "According to the reports I've heard, they were stolen en-route to the..."

"Freeton Antiquities Authority," offered Clarisse.

"The F-A-A," continued Dearth, the curl of a smile fanning his whiskers, "recovered two of the three cases, but they were empty. It would not be presumptuous to conclude the thief abandoned two cases and vanished with all six scrolls in the third. It was an Earth-dweller, one who knew the scrolls' worth. I believe they are not yet in Blodcroew's clutches."

"Just a regular thief?" asked Cary.

"In one of your own sayings, and one to which I am not overly fond; I smell a rat," smirked Dearth.

Gregory had slipped behind Dearth and was examining the handles of the sheathed knives crossed on Dearth's back. He sniffed. "Me too!"

Dearth spun round on Gregory as surprised as either Cary or Clarisse. The rat spy broke into a tittering laugh so peculiar it set Cary and Clarisse laughing, so that a moment later all four present were laughing. But their merriment was cut short. Large shadows, like giant moths scattered across the living room floor. All four cast their alarmed eyes to the windows. Ofost, Gren and Vaskar had arrived.

Clarisse motioned for them to fly to the back of the apartment to a large sash window in the kitchen.

In a flutter of wings, the Gildenhyrn were perched on the backs of three dining room chairs.

"Ascentors," said Vaskar, "Fyrndagas Underdel Dearth, we bear ill tidings. Mandwar..." The warrior paused. "Our Captain, Guardian of Husgard..." Vaskar faltered.

Gren took over. "Mandwar fell in the battle over the Golden Fields. Vaskar was witness. The Golden Vines caught him and bore him across the Mirror sea. Mandwar's Guardianship and the time passing for Shelter Island has ended."

"Where's the Mirror Sea?" asked Gregory, eyes large and round, looking from Vaskar to Gren, finally to Ofost. "Where did they take him?"

Ofost hopped to a chair nearer Gregory and spoke for his ears alone. "Mandwar has passed to the Realm of

Ellri," she whispered.

"Passed?" Gregory tensed. "Those are words Mom and Dad use when somebody dies—when Grandpa died—Did Mandwar die?"

Not a breath dared make a sound.

"He's dead—isn't he?"

Gregory ran to his bedroom, slamming the door behind him. Ofost fluttered after him.

"Even upon me," said Dearth, "who has borne much ill news over many times passing, this loss falls hard—but it falls hardest on tender hearts."

Cary and Clarisse sat down. Cary wondered what other sorrowful news Dearth might have heard in his long life. All fell quiet. Dearth remained by the doorway leading to the kitchen. Gren had taken position at the living room window to keep watch. Gregory's soft whimpering and Ofost's soothing entreaties floated through the room like a gentle mist.

The company was leaderless, as if mast and sails had been torn from their ship. Mandwar had always seen the dangers, known the way. A long minute passed. Discouragement settled over their thoughts like a blinding fog, as if they had flown into the Lost Veil.

Ofost returned looking uneasy. Her words had brought little comfort to Gregory.

Dearth's voice cut through the gloom.

"As is the custom, I am afraid the Guardianship of Fridorfold falls to me," he stated, as if recalling a past ceremony. "I would be glad it were not so. I am not as wise, nor as good-humoured as my friend. Perhaps, in time..."

Dearth stopped himself. He was not used to making

speeches, short or otherwise.

"As it stands," he continued, his voice now inhabiting the clarity and decisiveness they had come to trust, "as Mandwar has decreed, I am to Captain the Gildenhyrn—alongside the three Ascentors."

Bewildered, Vaskar, Ofost and Gren turned their attention to Dearth. Bird-folc had never been led by any other than a bird. Dearth was old past remembering to be sure, and Mandwar had hinted that Dearth had been present, though young, in times long past, and the Guardian Owl had named him successor should anything befall him. But not one creature, including Dearth, expected that day would come.

"For Fridorfold." It was Vaskar. He fanned his wings in affirmation.

"For Fridorfold," followed Gren and Ofost, each extending a wing.

"For Fridorfold," joined Cary and Clarisse, thankful that Mandwar's responsibilities had not wholly fallen on them.

"And Mandwar."

Gregory had returned, his tears still meandering down his red cheeks. His small voice had pushed through the last shadows of doubt like a rainbow.

"For Mandwar," the company declared, their eyes on Gregory, every inch a son of Mandwar.

"We must contact all creatures loyal to Fridorfold," said Dearth, placing a long paw over Gregory's shoulder. "We will muster the Gildenhyrn and pick up the trail of the scrolls."

"We will contact Bird-folc loyal to Fridorfold and the Gildenhyrn," offered Ofost, Gren nodding in agreement.

"I will hunt the scrolls," said Dearth, noting the puzzled look on Vaskar. "The Ascentor's parents have discovered scrolls of a time passing that may be of use to us, but they have been stolen."

"What should we do?" asked Cary.

"Brador Halar, Arithi, and Aevi," Dearth looked at Gregory, "You have the greatest task, a task I am certain Mandwar would have given you. You must find the Singer."

"The Singer?" asked Clarisse. "There's another Singer—like Adarel?"

"The one you seek is Keida," said Dearth. "She is as old as the Fragile Lands, as old as Fridorfold. When you find her, you will know what to do."

"But our parents are on their way home," objected Cary. "We can't just go on a field trip every day searching for..."

"Keida," repeated Dearth.

"Keida—not without telling them." Cary checked to Clarisse, then back to Dearth. "My dad won't believe any of this—I mean, anything that's happened to us, about Shelter Island and wings—and talking birds and a talking..."

"Rat?" grinned Dearth. "But search you must. Blodcroew will not rest. As we speak, the raven will be fortifying a new stronghold, hatching some new mischief."

"Our summer vacation starts in a few days," offered Clarisse. "Maybe we can ask to go to Grandma's."

Clarisse walked to Gregory and put her arm around him. "You'd like that, right Gregory?"

Clarisse appealed to Cary. "She lets us do almost anything we want, if we're back by dark."

"Why does my sister always have the best ideas?" said Cary. "We'll try."

"Where does your grandmother live?" asked Dearth.

"On a small farm—East, towards the mountains. It's a hobby farm—she makes honey—well, she doesn't make it. She looks after..." said Cary.

"She's an Apiarist," interrupted Clarisse.

"Near Cornerbrook," said Cary, raising a grin at having chipped in the last word.

Dearth addressed the company. "The matter is settled," he said. "Ten turns of the earth, look to the bees; look to the trees."